The

Reindeer

Keeper

The Reindeer Keeper

Believe Again...

BARBARA BRIGGS WARD

Illustrated by Suzanne Langelier-Lebeda

The Reindeer Keeper: Believe Again

Published by Wheatmark®
610 East Delano Street, Suite 104
Tucson, Arizona 85705 U.S.A.
www.wheatmark.com

In cooperation with:
The Maggie O'Shea Company
P.O. Box 627
Ogdensburg, New York 13669 U.S.A.
www.thereindeerkeeper.com

ISBN: 978-1-60494-443-3
LCCN: 2010923687

For my father

Chapter One

ABBEY READ OBITS AS IF THEY were short stories. To Abbey, they were. This queer obsession began years earlier when she'd sit at her father's desk in the funeral home and clip obituaries from the local newspaper. There'd be a copy for his files and copies for the family. The ones for the family were always clipped a little more neatly.

Abbey knew some paid her father what they could; not in money but rather in gifts of food or labor. The most amazing gift came from a most unlikely source. Abbey remembered the name when a lawyer phoned one February afternoon. She recalled the old man had been buried without fanfare. From his obit she learned he had no children or siblings. He'd been a recluse living somewhere off County Route 12. On a single sheet of lined paper, notarized and witnessed and in perfect penmanship, this stranger bequeathed all his worldly possessions to Abbey's father. This included a turn-of-the-century farmhouse, more than one hundred and twenty acres of woodland and meadows, and a cluster of outbuildings, including a barn set off by itself in a backfield.

Abbey asked the obvious. "Why?"

The lawyer answered matter-of-factly, "He was a loner. Most felt there was something peculiar about him, so when he never made any attempt to engage in small talk, no one bothered to take the first step. He was judged without anything to back it up."

Abbey's father often reminded her not to judge a book by its cover. It was making sense now.

"Whenever their paths crossed, your father always stopped the old man and started a conversation. He was sincere in asking how things were going or if he needed anything. This is all documented in the simple will, which includes his personal thanks to your father for being his friend."

Abbey wasn't surprised. Compassion was what drove the funeral director, even for those considered a bit odd.

"There's one more paragraph," continued the lawyer. "He writes that at the time of your father's death, everything as stated above is to go to you."

"Me? Why me?"

"He explains that although he never had the privilege of meeting you, he understood that you walk your father's path."

Stunned, Abbey told the lawyer, "I'll bring my father in to finalize the paperwork."

Upon hearing of the gift, Abbey's father cried—not out of joy but because he'd never be able to thank his friend. Sadly, this funeral director himself passed away a few months later. Abbey wrote his obit. She sat at his desk in the funeral home and clipped copies of his story from the newspaper. One was for his file. The others, clipped a little more neatly, were for his family.

Chapter Two

It was snowing again. Abbey was glad. With Christmas approaching, snow was on her checklist. The move in mid-November had been an easy one. All the furnishings stayed so it became a mingling of tastes when settling the old homestead.

Being a kindergarten teacher, Abbey was off for the holidays. Years back she knew someday she'd want to have a family. Choosing teaching made perfect sense. Besides, she loved being around the little ones who still possessed a wonder about the world.

"When will you retire?" some people now asked.

"They keep me believing," she'd answer. "Why would I give that up to sit and twiddle my thumbs?"

Steve felt the same way. It was part of the reason why they had such a good marriage after thirty-some years. He wasn't a golfer. He never fished, and hunting was out of the question. Both he and Abbey weren't travelers so buying a motor home and riding around did not interest them. He'd started the lumberyard when their firstborn, Eric, was two. Since then it had grown to include a garden/landscaping center and, just recently, appliances. It was a good life; although Steve was aware the big-box stores could move in any day and put an end to what he'd worked so hard to build. Abbey knew Steve worried more than he let on. And that kept Abbey awake at night.

Eric, now twenty-nine, hadn't been home in almost two years. Abbey was concerned about him. He was quite successful in the business sense, but the stress of Wall Street and a high-powered wife was taking its toll. Abbey read between the lines of their conversations. Meg had made a name for herself as the lawyer to retain when seeking settlements in malpractice suits. She was cutthroat. She demanded a good price and got it.

If anyone did any cooking in their overpriced apartment, it was Eric. Abbey used to think he might grow up to be a chef. He was always asking to help in the kitchen. He even collected cookbooks. Some were sitting with Abbey's on a shelf near the stove. Ironically when they moved, Steve had suggested she toss them out.

"I could never do that honey. Those cookbooks were part of Eric's childhood. There are memories attached to each one of them. I'd sooner throw away those now-tarnished silver platters we received as wedding gifts."

After that, Steve didn't question the fate of boxes of drawings Abbey had kept. Both their sons were always creating.

Sam actually pursued his childhood passion. Entrepreneurship carried him to Los Angeles. Filming documentaries took him around the world. He shared his life with Cate, a photographer he'd met while riding the rail from Paris to Spain. She caught Sam's fancy the minute she sat next to him. Abbey thought they should plant some roots, get married, and start a family while they were still young, but she never said a thing. She knew it was none of her business. This was a new generation. With the world at their fingertips, they had choices never thought possible back when she and Steve started out.

Because neither of the boys had been able to make it back for their grandfather's funeral, Abbey was overjoyed when they said they'd be home for Christmas. She was determined to make the few days they'd share as perfect as possible despite the fact it'd be her first Christmas without her father. He'd always spend Christmas Eve with them. He'd always cut the prime rib on Christmas Day. Besides dealing with her loss, Abbey worried Meg might get bored or that she and Cate wouldn't get along. They'd only met once, and only for a few hours. With their lives total opposites, Abbey feared her sons would have nothing to say to each other.

Steve kept telling her, "Relax. It will all work out."

So that's what Abbey tried to do, baking cookies and breads and freezing them until needed. She ordered a prime rib from the local butcher and went online for cheesecakes from their favorite deli in the city, all for Christmas dinner. She'd make the traditional recipes she made every year. She'd gone to the malls a few times looking for ideas but it was hard to buy for those who need nothing. Abbey had never been a big shopper. When Eric and Sam were young, she'd be running to stores in a panic right up to the twenty-fourth.

With only three days to go before they'd be home, Abbey and Steve finally walked the property. They were in a bit of a rush, behind schedule due to Steve working overtime. Not only were they looking for the perfect Christmas tree but boughs to make wreaths as well. Abbey was ecstatic when they found a pond already frozen.

"To think we own all this is humbling." Abbey snipped some low branches. "It hasn't sunk in yet."

"I feel the same way every time I drive into the place."

"I wish Dad could have enjoyed this, but he never would have moved out of his home."

"You knew him better than anyone Abbey."

"He invested so much time in trying to bring splintered families together. Yet, he was a skeptic when it came to today's technology, believing the more we are connected by devices, the more disconnected we'll become."

"Each generation has its thing."

"What was ours? The Beatles? Assassinations?"

"Flower power, honey. Baby boomers wore flowers in their hair, remember?"

Back then, they marched down Pennsylvania Avenue with a few thousand others protesting the Vietnam War. Steve, a senior at Kent State during the riots, had been on the front lines when it all broke loose. Tumultuous times defined them, although Abbey never really wore flowers in her ironed hair that reached down to her waist, nor did she go to Woodstock. Eric thought everyone went to Woodstock.

"There's something special about this place." Abbey had gathered enough boughs. She kept talking as they got serious about finding the tree. "I can't explain it. I just have a feeling."

"You and your feelings."

Without another word, Steve picked up the branches and piled them in the toboggan. The last time Abbey had a premonition she discovered the lump on her left breast a week later. Now in remission for over eighteen months, she was feeling better than ever. Steve was still having a hard time with her cancer. The thought of losing her was a place he refused to go. Just a month earlier, they'd buried their best friend's wife, only fifty-nine and full of it. Abbey cut the woman's obit out of the paper. She put a copy in her father's files, now kept near the bookshelves in the front room, and gave her friend's family as many as they needed.

"Look, honey. Over there." Steve pulled back some branches. "Now there's a tree."

Abbey needed a better view. Steve understood. He'd been through this process countless times. He knew the first question.

"Do you think it is tall enough? It looks so short."

"They always seem smaller in the woods."

"But do you think it's full enough?"

"The branches will come down once it's inside."

"Let's take a closer look."

When Abbey said that, Steve knew she liked it.

"It looks good all the way around. No brown needles. If you think it'll be big enough with those high ceilings, then this is the tree."

"It's full all right. I might need some help getting it to the house."

"I'll ask the caretaker. I've noticed he's at the barn early and stays 'til after dinner."

Steve marked their choice with a red ribbon. It was getting late. Abbey wanted to do more baking before dinner. Pulling the toboggan behind them, they made their way back home just as the snow started tumbling down.

Chapter Three

Besides the woods, the barn set far back in an open field was the other place Steve and Abbey hadn't explored. With work and settling in, they hadn't found the time. But that didn't mean they weren't curious. A clause in the old man's will specifically dealt with the imposing structure, home to a few sheep, about eight horses, and a herd of reindeer. Details stated the barn was not to be disturbed. It was to be kept in proper repair and the animals were to be allowed to "live, graze, and flourish without interruption in a routine established long before time." A caretaker had been appointed and he was "dutifully aware of his responsibilities—those that were obvious and those that were not." A trust fund for carrying out such terms was in the hands of the lawyer.

Abbey hadn't thought about what all that meant. She assumed the old man's reclusive lifestyle had a lot to do with it. He'd obviously bonded with the animals and probably thought of them as his family. When one dies it's natural to have everything in place for those left behind. Abbey had seen that over and over at the funeral home. Now with an oversized tree needing to be felled and brought inside, it was time to meet the caretaker.

It was still snowing a smidgen as Abbey headed out to the barn. The walk was invigorating. She hadn't realized how far it was from the house. Now up close, she got a better sense of the barn's massive size. The Green Mountains and quaint homesteads with picket fences far off in the distance provided the perfect backdrop. Peering inside, she didn't see the man she'd only noticed from afar. Abbey knew he was around somewhere. His truck was parked in the same spot it was every morning.

"Hello? Hello? It's the lady from the farmhouse. Hello?"

Once inside, Abbey slid the door shut and looked around. She wished Steve was with her. He would have loved the wood and architecture. Haylofts were brimming. A movement of sorts guided Abbey to another door. This one was slightly ajar. Peeking through the crack, Abbey was delighted by sheep scurrying after a cat that seemed to have the upper hand.

"They do this every morning, miss. It's a game they play before they're fed. I was hoping you'd stop in."

"I'm Abbey."

"I know."

"You know?"

"I read the will."

"I still don't understand why my father and I were chosen."

"In due time."

"How long have you been here?"

"I've been caring for the animals as far back as I can remember. Would you like me to show you around?"

"Yes, I'd enjoy that."

"My name is Thomas. Excuse the mess. It's a busy place this time of year."

Whatever it was about this man, Abbey couldn't put her finger on it. She couldn't understand much of what he said. He was shorter than he looked when driving in and out. He had to be up there; older than Steve, who was two years older than she was. His little, beady eyes gave him a serious look as he worked about the animals. He had a way with them. She watched as he spread the bales.

The cat followed Thomas as he led Abbey into a granary where sacks upon sacks were stored. Bins were loaded.

"You must go through a lot of hay over the winter?"

"Yes, Miss Abbey. Oats, too."

Opening another door, Thomas waited for Abbey to go first. She counted at least six of the eight horses in stalls.

"The others are outside," he explained.

Thomas motioned. He guided Abbey past a beautiful pinto and through yet another door which led them out behind the barn, hidden from view of the farmhouse and passersby.

"Breathtaking," remarked Abbey. "I've kept my eye out for them. How many?"

"This herd. About twenty."

"There are more?"

"Most certainly. There has to be."

The only reindeer Abbey had ever seen were from a distance. It was mid-August. They'd taken the boys to a family attraction in the mountains. Because of the humidity, the few reindeer present were hiding under any shade they could find.

"They've just been fed, Miss Abbey. They might get a little frisky." Thomas walked over to a smaller one standing off from the rest.

"Come meet the runt of the herd."

"They're so soft. Their antlers are amazing." Staying by the little reindeer, Abbey soon found herself surrounded by the entire herd. They weren't shoving. They seemed content.

"Reindeer can size a person up pretty quick. Looks like they sense your gentle spirit."

Lingering awhile longer, Thomas explained, "I must excuse myself. I have to get back to work. There's much to do these last few days."

That reminded Abbey to ask Thomas if he'd give Steve a hand with the tree.

"I saw the ribbon in the woods. I'll come a little earlier in the morning. Have your husband meet me here." Thomas took Abbey back to where she came in.

"It was a pleasure meeting you. I know you're busy. I have a long list today, too."

"Stop in anytime." Thomas went back inside. He mumbled something about a list, but she didn't catch it.

Abbey felt like a kid trudging through the snow. Her footsteps from earlier had disappeared. The thought of finding their ice skates and shoveling off that pond reminded Abbey how Sammy used to love skating on the creek behind her grandfather's place. Steve thought their youngest had the stuff to go pro but Sammy just wanted to have fun. Curiosity defined him even as a child. Such a rigorous structure would have been Eric's thing. Too bad he never took to sports. If Steve had his way, both boys would have played on some sort of team straight through high school just as he had done.

Past Christmases flashed through Abbey's mind as a cluster of chirping birds disappeared into a cedar hedge. From big wheels to BB guns, Christmas seemed to mark the boys' paths to maturity. The farther along they went, the more the wonder faded.

"Can't go back. It's just what happens," Abbey told herself. She picked up speed as the thought of a cup of coffee pushed her through the mounting drifts.

Chapter Four

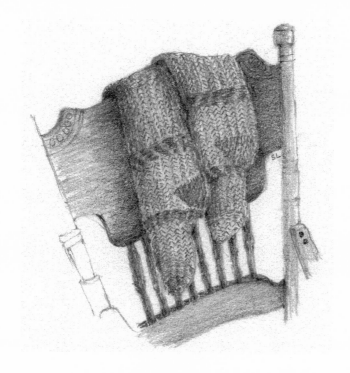

ABBEY COULDN'T BELIEVE HOW FAST THE time was flying. The next day became a blur of baking, wrapping gifts, and running to the store more than once. By the time Steve returned, he could tell she had reached her limit.

"Let's go into town for dinner," he suggested.

She didn't think she was that hungry until he mentioned their favorite restaurant, the sort of place where one could dress leisurely and still enjoy a fine entrée with a glass of wine. Before leaving, they decided to get the tree lights out and test them.

Opening the box, Abbey found the boys' Christmas stockings lying on top.

"I can still see you sitting by the window, knitting late into the evening, in a hurry to have the stockings ready for Santa. Why is it, Abbey, that when your kids are young, you think they'll be young forever?"

"I think it's because you're so busy you don't notice the clock ticking. We were raising the boys and growing the lumberyard at the same time. I still wonder if I should have been home more."

"We did our best. There's not a book written that can tell you how to raise a child."

"True. Many of the so-called experts have no children themselves." Abbey remembered what she wanted to ask. "What time's Thomas coming in the morning?"

"Seven. But something tells me it could be earlier. He was waiting for me today; told me he'd been at the barn before six." Shaking his head, Steve continued. "I thought I might lose him in a snow pile, but he forged right through. We had the tree up the back steps and on the side porch in stride. He's sort of an odd character. He left in a hurry, saying he had duties that needed tending."

"There is something curious about him."

"You were right about that barn. It's amazing, not your ordinary barn."

"It's definitely one of a kind." Abbey put the stockings on the back of a chair while they moved some furniture to make way for the tree. "Think we'll have enough lights?" she asked.

"I'll string the tree in the morning. If we need more lights, I can bring them back with me. Don't worry. The tree will be decorated by the time they get here. We still have another day to get things ready."

"I hope Sam's flight is on time. I haven't heard the forecast for the 23rd."

"I checked earlier. Clear through the twenty-eighth."

"Eric said if they can get in and out of LaGuardia without a hitch, they should be home around dinnertime."

Abbey was glad the boys would be arriving before Christmas Eve. That day would be hectic enough. After rearranging furniture and testing lights, the two went to dinner. They sat and talked until after ten.

Chapter Five

STEVE WAS RIGHT. THOMAS WAS KNOCKING on the back door at six forty-five. The tree was on the stand and in front of the bay window by seven thirty.

"Stay and have a cup of coffee. There's pumpkin bread made fresh yesterday."

"No, thank you, Miss Abbey. I must get going. If you don't mind, I'll take a slice with me."

"I'll wrap up a few. You must get hungry working so hard."

"It's not work."

"I remember you telling me that. I saw how much the animals care about you. They watch your every move."

"That's because I feed them. Now you have a way."

"A way?"

"Animals are intuitive. Reindeer do not gather around every stranger." After thanking Abbey for the bread, Thomas put his gloves on and started out the door. "The tree is where it's always been. I knew it would be. I knew it."

After watching the blowing snow devour Thomas, Abbey went to check on Steve stringing the lights.

She found him climbing down the ladder. "I'll be bringing more strands home, honey."

"It did look smaller out among so many." Abbey laughed. "You were right again."

"It's magnificent. You always pick out the perfect tree."

"*We* always pick out the perfect tree. I remember how the boys couldn't wait to get to the woods every December. I can't imagine going to the attic and bringing down a box of parts. I'm not ready to assemble branches."

"Searching for *the* tree has become a tradition."

"And now trees surround us. We're fortunate."

"That we are." Steve checked the time. "What's your plan for the day?"

"I want to get stockings for Meg and Cate and stuff to put in them. I'll stop at the grocery and then visit the cemetery. I have a wreath for Dad's headstone."

"Want me to go with you?"

"Thanks honey but it's something I have to do by myself. I can't explain it."

"You don't have to, Abbey. Call if you forget anything. I'll pick it up on my way. I'll be a little late. Have to do my shopping."

"Remember we agreed. Nothing expensive. I don't need a thing."

"You say that every year. Have you forgotten how we'd have to scrape enough money together to buy for the boys when they were little? We'd go without. Indulge me the pleasure to surprise you now."

Steve hurried out the door. He'd be busy today. Poinsettias and gift certificates were best sellers when Christmas was near.

Why she was always in the stores at the last minute baffled Abbey. Many of her fellow teachers had everything bought by October. Before Thanksgiving they had everything wrapped and their baking started. To Abbey, the rush was part of the season although she complained every year when trying to get it all accomplished. There wasn't much to send this year with the boys coming back. She had other relatives, like cousins, but they'd grown apart. It was sad after sharing so many holidays together. She'd invited her brother. Even though Jack was eight years older, they remained close. Abbey thought because their father had passed away, he'd want to be home for Christmas.

"There's no other place I'd rather be than with you this Christmas, Abbey. But Claire made arrangements for us to go to Hawaii. Have I told you about Claire? I think I have. I met her in Chicago about a year ago. She's the thirty-eight-year-old news anchor. Are you ready for this? We're getting married. I know what you're going to say Abbey, but this time it's the real thing."

"Will your children be with you?" Jack had three grown children scattered about the country.

"No. They have their own families. It's too hard to pack them up, presents and all. I'll call you Christmas, Abbey. I miss you. Give my love to everyone."

Abbey worried Jack would never find the right woman. She felt blessed to have found Steve.

Bargains were everywhere, as were the crowds. Abbey bought the perfect stockings and things to put in them. She picked up favorite wines and stocked up on staples. She had the skates sharpened. She hoped they'd fit. If Meg and Cate wanted to skate, she didn't know what they'd do. Steve told her not to worry, so she didn't.

Besides a few little things, Abbey decided that an enlarged photo of the boys when they were two and three, sitting under the Christmas tree, would be Steve's present. It had special meaning for sitting with the boys were her father and Steve. They were all laughing at a joke her father had told. She knew Steve would remember what was so funny. Her father's sense of humor always surprised people. Abbey felt it was a part of how he consoled those in the grieving process.

The cemetery was the last stop. Living above a funeral home afforded Abbey an appreciation of the rows upon rows of headstones. Each was like a shortened obit, offering a glimpse of a life. Infant to senior citizen and soldier to dignitary, it didn't matter. They all shared this final resting place. The funeral director was buried off the main roadway, under a maple tree overlooking a meadow that led to the foothills. He'd bought the lot years back.

Abbey's mother was buried beside him. She'd died from diabetes when Abbey was fourteen. That's what her father always said. But Abbey thought differently. She still did. It still hurt. There must have been another reason. Mothers weren't supposed to leave their families. Daughters need their mothers. The bitterness toward her mother was as strong as ever. It was the one subject Steve knew not to bring up.

The plow had only bothered to go halfway in. That was fine with Abbey. She came prepared. After checking her boots and tightening her scarf, Abbey was off to visit her father. She wasn't the only one to visit a loved one before Christmas. Scanning over the tops of the tombstones, Abbey noted the many wreaths and poinsettias already in place.

It was beautiful. The snow sparkled like crystals all about the gravesite. Rabbit tracks went around and around the maple and then disappeared into the field. Abbey took off a glove and wiped away what snow there was concealing his name. She knelt down and kept rubbing the letters with her bare hand. She told him how much he was missed and how much he was loved. She told him the boys were coming home. She told him she thought Jack wished he could be back home, too. Then she told him about the farmhouse, the barn, and its occupants.

"You should see the reindeer, Dad. They make me feel like a kid again. Remember the Christmas you took Jack and me to see Santa downstairs at that five-and-dime store? Remember, Dad? I was frightened. I cried and cried, so you sat on Santa's lap with me. You were a wonderful father. What you taught me, I carry with me every day."

Abbey wiped away the tears. After securing the wreath, she again rubbed her hand across his name while saying a prayer in silence. As she was leaving, the rabbits were back, running around and around the maple.

When Abbey opened the back door leading onto the sun porch she found a box from her cousin living in Utah and the cheesecakes she'd ordered. After hiding her day's purchases, Abbey started cooking. Although she knew Steve would take her out to eat again if she asked, the tree needed decorating and there was still a bit more wrapping and baking.

Once Abbey saw Steve's headlights coming down the driveway a few minutes after seven-thirty she quit worrying. He was later than she'd expected even when considering he'd been shopping.

"You must have bought the store out," kidded Abbey as he knocked his boots together to get the snow off.

"It was busy."

Noting the bags full of wrapped gifts, Abbey didn't think anything of Steve going upstairs without another word. After taking the casserole out of the oven, Abbey buttered the garlic bread and started to make a salad. But something was gnawing at her. She knew this man too well. That's why she called up the backstairs.

"Dinner will be ready in a few minutes. It'd be nice if we had a fire in the fireplace."

All Abbey heard in reply was the television. That was it. Up she went only to find Steve sprawled out on the bed. Presents were strewn about the room.

"Are you sick, honey? Can I make you some tea?"

"No."

"I made your favorite, macaroni and cheese. I figured I'd feed you before we tackle the tree."

"Not tonight, Abbey. Not tonight."

"That's okay. I can do the tree. I've done it before."

"Only once. I hadn't planned on that appendicitis."

Abbey sat at the end of the bed. "There's a lot we don't plan on. Tell me what's wrong."

He turned his head away. The north wind seemed to be getting stronger, whipping the snow up and around the gables.

Abbey moved a little closer and put her hand on his. "You can tell me Steve. You were my strength, the only reason I made it through losing our daughter only hours after she was born. You've been my rock through the cancer. You are my other half. When you hurt, I hurt."

"I don't want to ruin your Christmas."

"Christmas is but a day. Life doesn't stop happening because it's Christmas. Tell me. Tell me my love." She didn't like seeing Steve defeated. "Whatever it is, we'll get through it. We always have. Remember when you proposed? Remember? You got down on your knee in the freezing cold and told me there was nothing that could stop us. Nothing! I love you, Steve. You—"

Steve took Abbey in his arms and brought her down to the mattress. He kissed the nape of her neck, unleashed her hair held loosely in a ponytail, and brought his lips to hers. They made love as that wind kept teasing the windowpanes. The clock ticking on the mantle woke them up a bit later.

Wrapped in Steve's arms, Abbey whispered, "They're coming in, aren't they?"

"Plans have been ratified. The big guys break ground early spring. Grand opening is sometime late fall. How do we compete against them? So many work for us and depend on us Abbey. I don't know if we'll make it."

"You are a survivor Steve. You've grown a solid business based on customer satisfaction. You'll not only survive, you'll thrive."

"You believe that, don't you?"

"I believe in you. I always have."

So dinner was later than usual. It didn't matter. Steve built a fire as Abbey brought the casserole and trimmings into the front room with the bay window.

"Wine with this fancy meal?"

"Don't mean to be a party pooper, but I'd love a glass of milk."

"I'll make that for two."

The tree did get decorated between laughter, tears, and a few more glasses of milk. Each ornament brought back a memory that spurred conversation. At exactly one ten in the morning, the angel was in place.

"She'd be twenty-five this January, an Aquarius like her mother. Bet our little girl would have been a beauty." Steve turned out the lights and took Abbey's hand.

"We are blessed. We have an angel in heaven watching over us."

The wind hadn't let up and neither had the passion. They finally fell asleep around two.

Chapter Six

"Wake up, sleepyhead. The boys are coming home!"

For a second, what Steve was saying worked its way into what Abbey was dreaming. Then reality hit. It was the 23rd! The boys would be home for dinner. Meg and Cate would be under the same roof. Abbey sat straight up in bed.

"There's a cup of coffee for you on the stand." Steve was showered and ready to go. "I have to get there early."

Leaning down he whispered, "Thanks for getting me through last night. Love you. I'll call later." Steve kissed the top of her head and headed out the bedroom door. "Put the presents I brought home under the tree. And no peeking."

Minutes later, Abbey heard the truck running and Steve scraping the windshield. Rolling over, his warmth made her miss him already. She'd put up a good front last night but deep down, she was worried. She'd never tell him, but she was worried sick. What would he do? He'd started the lumberyard from scratch. Not even the banks believed in it at first. When he expanded to include the home and garden center, many thought he was foolish.

"Why ruin a good thing?" they questioned.

Steve followed trends. He kept track of those giants eating up one small business after another, community after community. But rumor is nothing like reality. Once the opening date had been set, that reality paralyzed Steve. Abbey was thankful he'd confided in her instead of keeping it to himself until after the holidays. They were a partnership. It wasn't easy at times, especially when that partnership became lopsided. But that's when communicating kicked in. So many they knew had divorced. Some, like Jack, had it happen more than once.

She stayed there, wrapped in her favorite quilt going over what she had to do. She'd check the weather and call Eric. She wanted everything done by the time they arrived. She and Steve decided not to tell the boys about the lumberyard. There was no need to. They had their own lives to contend with. When the clock announced six forty-five, Abbey jumped out of bed.

Now showered and dressed, Abbey stood looking out the kitchen window. She'd called Eric. If all went as planned, they'd be home for dinner. Standing there, she felt drawn to the barn. Before starting her day, Abbey fixed a tray of cookies and set off to find Thomas.

The snow was deeper than when she last visited. This time, she went right in. She knew the way. She walked past the sheep still being teased by that cat. Most of the horses were outside. There was no sign of the reindeer. Abbey noted the hay had been laid where needed. Another door caught her attention, one she hadn't noticed before. It was closed but that didn't stop her. She slowly pulled it open. The sight of reindeer everywhere startled her.

"I knew you'd stop by. Come in. Come in."

"Thomas, there are so many reindeer."

"Has to be."

Unsure of what he meant, Abbey continued, "I brought you some cookies. And if you happen to be taking care of the animals tomorrow night, stop in and meet our children. You are welcome to stay for dinner."

"Thank you, Miss Abbey. Thank you. But I'm always booked on Christmas Eve."

"I know it's a night for family."

"Most certainly."

"Do you have family in the area?"

"No, they're far away. But they visit every Christmas Eve."

"Good. No one should be alone on Christmas."

Thomas stopped what he was doing to try a cookie. "Coconut, one of my favorites. Someone else I know makes great cookies, too. She bakes all year for Christmas."

"She must have a big family."

"Biggest one ever."

Abbey looked about the reindeer. "How do you feed all of them?"

"One at a time."

"This barn is immense."

"Has to be."

"Each reindeer has its own space?"

"Definitely."

"Mind if I look around?"

"I hoped you would."

"Their coats are so soft." Abbey kept talking as she went from one reindeer to the next. "Their antlers are majestic. It's as if they are waiting for something-or someone."

"'Tis the season Miss Abbey. 'Tis the season for sure."

The tone in Thomas' voice made Abbey turn back around and look at him. In that split second she felt like a child waiting in anticipation. Except for a window creaking up in the hayloft, it was silent.

"Would you like to feed the runt Miss Abbey?"

Abbey couldn't shake the moment.

"The runt Miss Abbey. Would you like to feed her"?

Whatever it had been, Abbey was beyond it now. "Yes. Yes Thomas I'd love to feed her. How much?"

"You'll know."

Thomas was right. She filled the feeder a little over half and quit.

"Perfect." Thomas then handed Abbey a brush.

"I can brush her?"

"She's yours."

The runt stood still as Abbey groomed her. "I wish I could stay with you all day wee one. You are so beautiful. Merry Christmas sweetheart."

Abbey found Thomas filling buckets of water. She explained she had to get back home. "That dinner invitation stands although I know you'll be with family."

"The runt doesn't stay still for just anyone Miss Abbey." With a twinkle in his eye, Thomas continued with his work.

As she walked back to the house Abbey found herself remembering a doll with long braids she'd received one year for Christmas. She hadn't thought of that doll in years. It had been her favorite.

A phone ringing inside hurried her up the back steps.

"Where have you been?" asked Steve. "Sleeping after what I put you through last night?"

"I don't know what you're talking about. I enjoyed myself immensely."

"As did I, although I don't think I can drink another glass of milk for a while."

After Abbey told Steve when she expected the boys, he had to cut their conversation short.

"The place is mobbed," he explained. "Better enjoy the business while we can. I'll try to be home before they get there."

Abbey thought the boys would stay longer, but, with hectic schedules, Eric said they'd be leaving on the twenty-sixth.

"Be happy for the time you'll have," Abbey told herself as she pulled back the curtains in the front room for more light.

That's when she noticed the mailman driving away. Buttoning her sweater, Abbey hurried out the door only to find a few after-Christmas sale flyers and a letter from her doctor. She grabbed the newspaper along with the mail and headed back inside. Once she checked the ham, Abbey took her coffee and paper upstairs.

"Still clear," she thought looking out the window. "I'll freshen up and then make dessert."

Sitting on the bed, Abbey opened the paper, and found herself drawn to a familiar name printed on the obituary page. It was the obit of a close friend from high school.

Died December 21. Death caused by massive head injury in a two-car collision.

"Just like that," Abbey thought.

Leaving behind a husband, four children, and six grandchildren.

Abbey picked up the phone and ordered flowers. With three hours remaining, she spent the time in the kitchen. She'd left the unopened letter from her physician on the counter. After Steve's news, she wasn't in the mood for more.

While preparing ingredients for the caramel sauce, Abbey remembered telling Steve, "Whatever it is, we'll get through it."

She didn't mean the cancer. Losing the lumberyard would be one thing, but she wasn't ready to endure more radiation and chemo. She'd thrown up enough. A knock at the door interrupted her anxiety. It was one of Abbey's students.

"Marissa! What a surprise! Come in."

"I made this for you."

The little girl presented Abbey with an envelope decorated in crayon and glitter. Then she turned to leave.

"Wait, Marissa! I have some cookies for you."

After wrapping them in foil, Abbey put the cookies in a paper bag and handed it to Marissa. She also gave her one to eat. "Thank you for the beautiful card. I hope you and your family have a wonderful Christmas."

"Bye Mrs. Williams," smiled Marissa, taking a bite. "I like your cookie."

Abbey waved to Marissa's mother waiting in the car. The poor woman had so much to contend with that Abbey worried if she'd make it. Her husband had recently suffered a stroke. One of their two boys was severely autistic, and to make matters worse they were without health insurance. Steve and Abbey had recently gone shopping for the family.

Marissa's mom couldn't stop crying when they delivered the gifts.

Abbey told her, "It's the least we could do. The gifts are to be from Santa Claus."

Abbey sat down. As she opened Marissa's card, glitter spilled out onto the table. A reindeer with very tall legs, a very small body, and antlers resembling stalks of celery dominated the front. Inside were all sorts of hearts. There was no message. It didn't need one.

Looking at the crayon reindeer was the push Abbey needed to open that other letter. With one rip, Abbey was reading that her next checkup had been rescheduled. Included were slips for routine tests and blood work. She'd wait until the boys left to have the lab work done. She marked the change on the calendar and put the word "cancer" in the desk drawer for the time being.

After preparing items for the sauce, Abbey took one more glance around. The farmhouse mirrored that of a page out of one of those magazines she'd browse through while waiting in the grocery line. It still seemed as if they were visitors. Maybe having Eric and Sammy home would change that feeling. Abbey looked out the back door. The silver moon had turned the backfield into a bed of diamonds. She noted Thomas was still at the barn. Unfamiliar headlights coming down the driveway captured her attention. Her heart quickened. The boys were home for Christmas.

Without a coat, Abbey rushed out the door and down the steps. So excited, she didn't notice Steve driving in behind them. It was quite a scene in ten-degree weather, hugs, tears, and a scramble for luggage and presents to get inside the house. They were all talking at once. Abbey kept telling her boys how good they looked while thinking how tired Eric seemed.

"It might have been the long drive," she told herself.

She made a conscious effort to include Meg and Cate as she showed everyone into the front room.

"Great tree, Mom. I bet it took forever to pick out," said Sam.

"So you do remember all those Christmas tree escapades." Steve laughed.

"My favorite was the year you put two trees together because one wasn't full enough," commented Eric.

"Having the perfect tree makes the holiday," Abbey spoke.

"Hear this, Meg? This is where I get it," said Eric.

"Get what?" Abbey found herself reacting.

"Eric is upset with me because I insist on an artificial tree." Meg explained. "We're never home. We don't have the time to run around the city looking for one."

"Everyone has their traditions. Our first Christmas was a disaster. Steve's family never put their tree up until Christmas Eve. My family, it was at least two weeks before. After that first year, we compromised. We aim for the week before, although this year was a rush."

"From what I could tell, trees surround this place. It looked like a lot of woods when we drove in. All of that go with the house, Dad?" asked Sam.

"All of it. There's even a pond."

"I can't believe some stranger left this to you."

"We still can't believe it either. There's a barn, even some outbuildings."

"No strings attached? He just thought you and Grandpa were nice people, Mom?" Eric asked.

"Dad took him under his wing. He didn't have any family. He must have considered your grandfather the next best thing. The will gave specifics about caring for the animals, but other than that, it's ours."

"This home is amazing," spoke Cate. "Mind if I take some photos while we're here?"

"Our home is your home. Take all the photos you want," replied Steve.

"Let me show you your rooms. You can freshen up while I get dinner on the table."

"I smell your famous ham, Mom. Did you make your potatoes, too?"

"I did, Eric. And the applesauce."

"If you don't mind, I'll just have a salad. I forgot my tea. Would you have any?"

"I have your favorite teas, Meg," replied Abbey, "and a salad made."

Steve hung the coats and stoked the fire while Abbey led everyone upstairs. She'd added some feminine touches to make the girls feel like they weren't sleeping in a dorm.

Back downstairs Abbey searched for the tea bags and added more to the salad. About to take the ham out of the oven, she looked up and found Eric watching her.

"Let me get the ham, Mom. I never spend any time in a kitchen anymore."

Abbey again didn't say what she wanted to say.

"Here's the platter."

"You still have it. That's the one you've used every Christmas."

"The surroundings may be new, but everything else is the same."

"I've noticed. It feels like home."

That was what Abbey needed to hear. With Eric's few words, this marvelous gift from a stranger was now theirs.

"Pineapples are perfect." Eric eyed the ham as intently as a food critic would. After placing the meat on the platter, he asked, "Want it on the counter?"

"Yes, right here. You can take the potatoes out if you'd like."

"I haven't had potatoes like these since you last made them."

"I can give you the recipe."

"By the time I get home, it's time to go to bed. Meg gets home even later."

"What do you do about dinner?"

"It's whatever we grab. I prefer cereal. Meg sticks with her salad, if anything at all."

"You should cook on the weekends for the week. You have to eat."

"Lunch is takeout. I change it up."

"Doesn't that get expensive?"

"We don't buy groceries. It's a wash."

Taking a bowl from the cupboard, Abbey again held back. Sometimes it's the wise thing to do. They were only home for a few days. Why cause problems?

"Are you making that ham sauce, Mom?"

"Would you like to make it?"

"I would!"

"Go right ahead."

As Eric cracked the eggs he remarked, "This is your mom's bowl."

"How did you remember?"

"The crack. It has a little crack. I used to think that when I'd break open eggs, I'd break the bowl. It has to be ancient."

"It goes back a few generations. I only use it during the holidays."

"Did your mom do that? Save it for the holidays?"

"I don't know, Eric. It's what I choose to do."

That was it for any discussion about her mother. Eric knew to change the subject.

"I don't believe it!"

"What?"

"Up on the shelves! Are those my old cookbooks?"

"Some of them. The rest are in the attic."

"You kept all of them?"

"Of course I did."

"I was just a kid, Mom."

"They say that what you like doing when you are a child is where your passion for life lies."

"Even if I wanted to, I couldn't get off the merry-go-round I'm on."

"No matter what the situation, don't ever think you're stuck. Once you make a decision, things fall into place."

"This is a sight for sore eyes," Steve interrupted, "the two of you cooking together."

"It feels good, Dad. Mom was telling me you kept all my cookbooks."

"True, along with everything you and Sammy ever wrote, drew, or scribbled," Steve joked.

"I heard my name. Something smells delicious. I can't remember our last sit-down meal."

"Don't tell me you and Cate skip dinner, too?"

"We don't skip it. We just don't get to it 'til about ten most nights."

"You go to bed with a full stomach?" Eric asked.

"We get to bed about two, usually up working."

Snap! Cate snuck in and took a picture.

"Watch out for her. She'll show up out of nowhere."

Sammy grabbed the beautiful young woman with a long, reddish braid and twirled her about the kitchen.

"Don't mean to interrupt, but I'd like that tea now. I have a splitting headache."

"The water is hot, Meg. Do you need milk or sugar?"

"Nothing but tea."

"Why don't you relax by the fire?" Abbey handed Meg her tea. "Steve just has to carve the ham. You must be starving."

"Not really," Meg replied. Noticing Eric at the stove, she asked him what he was doing.

Before he could reply, she was gone.

"Need any help, Mom?" asked Sam.

"You could wrap the rolls in this basket and put them on the table. Then, light the candles."

"I'll keep taking pictures. There's so much going on," said Cate.

"There certainly is," replied Abbey, miffed by Meg's curt question.

"Let it go, honey."

Steve was right. That was the cold and selfish Meg they'd come to know. Abbey wondered what her oldest son had ever seen in her.

Once the ham was on the table, Eric went to get Meg.

"She's sound asleep. She does that a lot once she finally gets home."

"Snowing again." Steve had opened the back door. Between the fireplace and the oven, he wanted a little fresh air.

"Whose truck?" Sam noticed the lights going down to the barn.

Abbey talked about Thomas as they gathered for their meal. She found she could go on and on. She had that feeling again.

"Sammy, I'm thrilled we came. Snow and reindeer make for a perfect Christmas." Cate filled her plate with ham as the others said grace.

They sat around the table, enjoying good food and conversation. Sam talked about his travels to New Zealand to document the Maori culture.

"I like to get to the root of where things begin, where people get their ways of doing what they do."

"Sounds fascinating. In the process, you see the world," said Steve.

"I see it through the lens. My hope is that bringing the world to those who might never see what I'm shooting will foster an understanding they'd otherwise never gain."

"That's a big undertaking."

"It is, Mom, but you have to start somewhere. We all share the same planet."

"You remind me of my father. He'd try to bring families together when there'd been a death after they'd spent years apart."

"Did he succeed?" asked Eric.

"Occasionally, but too many times the split was impossible to heal no matter how hard he tried."

"Strange, isn't it?" spoke Sam. "We get but a short time here on earth, and we spend a lot of it in anger against those we are bound to."

"It's not that simple. I wish it were," added Eric. "Relationships can get complicated."

"I'm just glad I took that train," spoke Cate. "Otherwise, I never would have met my Sammy. Now we travel the world."

"Think you'll stay in California?"

"For now, it serves the purpose. Cate has freelance opportunities. But you never know. We talk of the Rockies or maybe Morocco or maybe New Zealand. The world is open to consideration."

"Come stay with us. You can document greed and power … on Wall Street, I mean," joked Eric.

Everyone laughed except Abbey.

Changing the subject, Sam commented, "I'm stuffed. That was delicious, Mom."

"No holiday meal is complete without something sweet. Tonight, it's rice caramel pudding with homemade whipped cream. Everyone want coffee?"

Noting four coffees and one tea, Abbey went into the kitchen. Eric followed.

"Mind if I whip the cream?" he asked.

"I love having an assistant."

Sam and Cate cleared the table. It didn't take long before the coffee was poured and the dessert was ready.

"This is so good," complimented Cate. "I've never had this before."

"This is one of Mom's traditions I told you about. I bet we have prime rib on Christmas," said Sam.

"Yes, we will." Abbey smiled. "And cheesecakes from the city."

"It's good to know you can count on some things remaining in place," commented Eric.

Noticing Sam and Cate looking toward the archway, Eric turned around. Meg was approaching the table.

"What are you referring to, Eric?"

"I meant traditions. Things you remember growing up. We live in such a rat race, Meg, that there's no time to enjoy the day."

"We choose to live in that race. Where else can you make what we make? Mind if I get some salad?"

"You sit next to Eric," spoke Abbey. "I'll get your salad. Would you like some ham? A few rolls?"

"No, the salad is fine."

Once Meg joined them, the conversation took on a guarded tone.

"What's the plan for tomorrow? It is Christmas Eve, after all!" Sammy was like a little boy in so many ways.

"It's whatever the four of you would like to do."

"I'd like to walk the property. You said there was a pond?"

"We did, Sam, and it's frozen," explained Steve.

"That's what I was hoping. Do you know where my skates are?"

"They're hanging up in the back kitchen. I had them sharpened."

"You knew, didn't you, Mom?"

"I knew that if you had the time, you'd go skating. What size are you, Cate?"

"I've never skated."

"It's easy, Cate. I'll show you." Sam smiled.

"I'm a size eight, or eight and a half with heavy socks, probably."

"You can use my skates," said Abbey. "I'd like to take everyone to the barn at some point-if you'd like to see it."

"I have to go to town. Maybe while you go see those animals," added Meg.

"You don't want to see the reindeer? It's Christmas, Meg."

"You know I never got into the Santa Claus thing, Eric."

"You didn't believe in Santa Claus?" Abbey asked.

"My parents divorced when I was two. I went from one to the other for the holidays. I'd ask every year up until I was about seven for Santa Claus to give me my family back. He never did. I quit believing."

That was the most Meg had ever said at one time—and the most revealing. After the table was cleared and the kitchen cleaned up, they sat around the tree enjoying a glass of wine. That's when there was a knock at the door.

It was Thomas. "I'm glad you stopped Thomas."

"Can't be staying, Miss Abbey. Might you have more of those coconut cookies?"

"Yes, indeed. Come in and meet our family."

Steve made the introductions while Abbey went to the kitchen. She was back in minutes.

"If you'd like more, just ask. I've told everyone about the reindeer. We thought we'd make a visit tomorrow."

"'Tis fine, 'tis fine. Best come early. It will be getting busier later on."

"We'll be out of your way by noon."

"Good-bye, everyone." The little man left as quietly as he came.

"He is a character, Mom. Just like you said," spoke Eric.

"I hope he lets me photograph him. He has interesting features," added Cate.

"He gives me the creeps." Meg's remark drew no response.

They stayed gathered about the tree until after midnight. Outside the snow kept falling. Later, lying in bed, Abbey found herself thinking about Eric's questions of how her mother celebrated Christmas and what traditions she herself carried on. Abbey remembered nothing. After hearing what Meg revealed, she understood the young woman a bit more. In a way she felt close to Meg. In the perfect world, families remain intact. In reality, too many intangibles come into play. Abbey had a hard time falling asleep.

Chapter Seven

STEVE WAS STACKING WOOD WHEN ABBEY made it down to the kitchen.

"You're wide-awake," remarked Abbey as he came through the back door. "I'm making coffee. Would you like a cup?"

"No thanks honey. I thought I'd get an early start. Try to let everyone go by two. You okay, Abbey? You were restless most of the night."

"I think I was on overload."

"When you're on spring break, how about we take some time and get away?"

"Maybe," Abbey replied, hugging Steve. "Let's wait and see where we're at."

Steve knew what she meant. "Call if you've forgotten anything."

Back outside, Steve did some more shoveling. As Sam came into the kitchen, Abbey could hear Steve's truck going down the driveway.

"Coffee's ready Sammy. Do you still like it black?"

"Thanks, Mom but I think I'll go for a run first."

"Mind if I tag along, Sam?" It was Meg speaking.

"Great. I was worried I might get lost in a snow bank."

Abbey watched the two sprint out of sight, thinking how especially beautiful Meg looked with her hair down, casual underneath her wool hat. She hadn't applied any makeup yet she radiated. Something seemed to be agreeing with her.

Eric was the last one up. Cate was already outside. The natural light afforded her endless photo opportunities.

"I've been thinking, Mom. I could cook on the weekends."

"It's a start. You always wanted to be a chef."

"Meg would never go for that. We have too much on our backs."

"One step at a time Eric. Don't be afraid of change."

After breakfast was served and Steve returned they visited Thomas. Meg decided to go into town later in the day.

Heading out the back door, Sam asked about Thomas.

"Does he ever leave? His truck is always parked in the same place."

"He tells me this is the time of the year when he's the busiest," said Abbey.

"What is he doing differently than any other day in a barn?"

"I have no clue, Sammy. According to Thomas, he has a long list and checks it off as he goes."

"Sounds like someone you used to tell us about this time of year," kidded Eric.

"My thought exactly." Abbey followed Steve right up to the barn door.

After Cate took some shots, they went inside.

"I've never been in a barn. Doesn't smell as bad as I thought it would," said Meg.

"That's because Thomas keeps it spotless," explained Abbey.

Cate kept snapping as Abbey led them by the sheep and horses. She hesitated when Abbey told her they were about to see the reindeer.

"I won't take any more," whispered Cate. "I don't want to startle them."

"Can't startle them young lady." Thomas looked up, not surprised to see his visitors coming through the door. "They're well-behaved. They have to be."

"You don't mind if I take a few pictures?"

"Don't mind at all. You won't be the first to try."

"I've never seen a reindeer," confessed Meg.

"Bet you have," remarked Thomas.

"They are magnificent, Thomas," commented Eric. "They must be a lot of work."

"Worth it for sure."

"Can we brush the runt?" asked Abbey.

"Most certainly, Miss Abbey. She's over there. Her brush is in with her."

They stayed longer than planned. Abbey again invited Thomas for dinner. Again, he explained he was expecting his family.

"There's something spellbinding about being in a barn full of reindeer on Christmas Eve." Cate's eyes were wide with wonder as she followed everyone out of the barn.

Abbey noticed boughs ready to be hung stacked by the door. "Decorating Thomas?"

"It's for the animals. They like to celebrate, too."

"Hope to see you tomorrow."

"Maybe sooner, Miss Abbey. Maybe sooner."

"This place looks like a Christmas card. I can't stop taking pictures."

As they headed back to the house, Steve suggested, "Cate, why don't you download your photos?"

"I definitely will after we go skating. What time are we leaving for church?"

"We should leave by eleven to get a seat," explained Abbey.

"Mom, I'd like to go to the cemetery. There's no telling when we'll be back. Do people go to cemeteries on Christmas?" asked Eric.

"Yes, people go to cemeteries on Christmas."

"Is Grandpa buried next to your mother?"

"Yes; your grandfather bought a plot."

"How old were you when you mother died?" Meg asked.

Abbey decided to keep her engaged, despite the topic. "I was fourteen."

"That must have been hard."

"I don't remember much. It's still a blur."

"I feel I lost my parents when they divorced."

"That must be hard."

"I try avoiding them. I feel my mother is the one most responsible."

Abbey understood. How could she advise when she herself felt such animosity toward her own mother?

Hesitating, she suggested, "We could go to the cemetery in the morning. Your grandfather would like that."

That was the plan.

After a light lunch, Meg asked Eric to go into town with her while Sam took Cate skating.

When they all returned, Abbey served hot chocolate while Steve built the fire. That's when the stockings were noticed.

"You did this, didn't you, Mom?" asked Sam.

"I don't know what you are talking about."

"You hung the stockings. I recognize two. The other two must be for Cate and Meg."

"We'll have to wait for morning to find out."

As Abbey brought out the good china, Cate came rushing into the room.

"You won't believe this. None of the reindeer pictures took. Not a one!"

"It must have been the lighting, honey."

"That's all I can think of Sammy. I'm so bummed."

While setting the table Abbey recalled Thomas' reply to Cate when asked if she could photograph the reindeer. "You wouldn't be the first who tried." He knew they couldn't be photographed.

"But why?" she wondered to herself.

Besides the china, crystal goblets and glass ladles were in place. Once the candles were lit, they sat down to enjoy the Christmas Eve feast. Even Meg couldn't resist the meal. And when Eric's carrot cake was served with lemon sauce drizzled on the top, Meg was the first to compliment him.

Later, presents were put under the tree, and to Abbey's delight, everyone went to the Christmas Eve service. They called it a night around two.

Chapter Eight

ABBEY TRIED TALKING HERSELF INTO FALLING asleep, but it was another one of those nights. By two thirty-five she'd made a cup of tea and
was sitting on the sofa. The moon shimmering through the darkness lit
the room, drawing her attention to a particular photo set back on a shelf.
Putting the cup down, Abbey went over and stood staring at her parents
on their wedding day. Even in the shadows, Abbey couldn't deny how
beautiful a woman her mother had been. Smiling, with her dark hair
pulled back and a veil of lace falling past her shoulders to her small waist,
this woman dressed in satin was looking at her husband with obvious
love in her eyes. He, in return, was infatuated with his bride.

From nowhere came tears. From nowhere came a yearning for this
stranger who'd carried her for nine months and delivered her on a cold
January morning. From what Abbey had been told, the labor had been
drastically long. Her father thought he might lose his wife. After the
birth, doctors told them it'd be wise not to have any more children.

Abbey used her finger to clear away any dust from the photo to get
an even better look. Many used to tell Abbey she resembled her mother
but she never acknowledged such claims until this moment. Staring at
her mother, whom she'd convinced herself she hated but now admitted
she never knew, was like staring straight into a mirror.

Out of the corner of her eye, Abbey noticed a sudden brightness
coming from outside. At first she thought it was the shimmering moon
among the silver stars. But the brightness intensified so that it drew Ab-

bey to the far window overlooking the backfields. Colorful sparkles were swirling over the land. Between the snow falling and the moon dancing, it was a sight that took her breath away. Abbey's attention turned to the barn. It was lit up as she'd never seen before. She knew Thomas was there. He had to be.

Abbey put the photo down and went to the back door. Without any thought, she opened it and walked down the steps and through the snowdrifts, with no coat, boots, or hat. She wasn't cold. She didn't even notice the snow twirling about her face and the below-zero temperature freezing the landscape. When she reached the barn, she didn't have to open the door. Thomas was waiting.

"Welcome Miss Abbey. We've been waiting for you."

Inside the barn, Abbey followed Thomas past the sheep and horses. He stopped in front of the door leading to the reindeer.

"Do you believe, Miss Abbey? Do you believe?"

Abbey understood what he was asking. Right there, she let go of her worries and sorrows. Gone were the cancer and thought of losing a business built from nothing. Gone were anxieties over Cate and Sam settling down and Eric and Meg divorcing. Gone was the sadness over the loss of her child. Gone was a daughter grieving her father and hating her mother.

Abbey found herself thinking back to a Christmas forgotten. She was four. Dressed in a flannel nightgown, she was sitting in front of a Christmas tree decorated with mostly ornaments she and Jack had created. Her stocking was in her lap. Jack was beside her. Even though he was older, he was still a believer. Their parents sat watching them. One gift excited Abbey more than the rest. It was a painting of Abbey in her favorite sundress playing with her kittens. She jumped up to hug her mother. Her mom had been the artist. Abbey remembered that summer day. Sunshine was all around while she sat playing with her kittens in the backyard.

Standing in that barn, Abbey could smell the flowers in the garden her mother tended, the lilacs and lilies of the valley and snapdragons mingling with tulips. She could see her mother patiently waiting for her to stay put so she could sketch her daughter on canvas. She could hear her mother tell her how beautiful she looked in her new dress with kittens all around. She remembered her mother. She remembered.

"I believe, Thomas. I do believe."

A faint jingling of bells broke the silence. Abbey walked behind Thomas as he opened the door to the reindeer stall and stepped inside. Those glittering crystals were everywhere. This portion of the barn was an astonishing sight with fresh boughs of cedar and pine wrapped about wooden posts and wreaths hung in front of windows up high. Standing in the midst of it all was a most splendid Christmas tree. Wild berries and acorns were strung around its branches. All the while, the jingling was getting louder. The reindeer were getting anxious. Barn cats hid.

After motioning for Abbey to stay by the tree, Thomas approached the back of the stall, which was more door than wall. Thomas took a last look about and slid the latch up. Then he pushed with all his might. At first, it didn't move, but, as those bells grew louder, the door opened. The swirl of crystals increased. Staying put, Abbey could still see the stars. They looked so low as if they were touching the earth. Stirring snow filled the night air. The jingling stopped. A hush blanketed the night as Santa Claus stepped into the barn.

He was taller and plumper than Abbey had ever imagined. His beard was whiter, fuller than any mall Santa's beard could ever be. His cheeks were a deep red, as was his velvet suit. With a shiny black belt, shiny black boots, and a smile as warm as summer, Santa approached the reindeer. Abbey watched as he spent time petting each one while checking the might of their antlers and width of their legs.

Inside came elves in a hurry, carrying packages that they placed under the tree. Others carried in a tray piled high with cookies. Soon all the elves gathered around Thomas. Abbey heard one little elf call Thomas "Papa." She realized the elves were Thomas' family.

After visiting the last reindeer, Santa pointed to one and then another. Some of the older elves led those particular reindeer outside and hitched them up to the sleigh. By observing what was going on, Abbey understood these were not ordinary reindeer kept inside this barn. They were groomed to be Santa's reindeer. Abbey strained to see more, just as she had done when looking out her bedroom window atop the funeral home in search of his sleigh. She was so intent that she didn't notice Santa standing by her side.

"I remember when you were five years old, Abbey. I was maneuvering the sleigh around all those trees your father cared for dearly. I saw you sound asleep in your window seat. You must have been waiting a long time. Your mother came as I was landing. She picked you up and tucked you into bed. Now come with me. I will show you the sleigh."

Santa led Abbey outside. Despite being in her nightgown and bare feet with snow falling, Abbey was still warm as toast. Her amazement of being in the presence of Santa Claus on Christmas Eve was obvious.

The sleigh was massive. Leather reins trimmed with bells lay on the seat. Filling the back was that bag full of toys. The reindeer seemed anxious to get going. They knew this was the night.

"Sit with me, Abbey. I want to talk to you before I go."

Santa climbed aboard, held out his hand, and pulled Abbey up. Over the fields, church bells echoed in the distance.

"A perfect night. A bit of a wind, but it's behind me. Thomas has done such a fine job with the reindeer this year. I'll be home in record time."

"What does Thomas do, Santa? Why don't you keep your reindeer at the North Pole?"

"I knew you'd have questions. As a child, you always had spunk about you. You always tried staying awake on Christmas Eve while Jack fell sound asleep. Truth is, the reindeer chosen for the flight need to experience more than just winter. I travel the world. They need to be able to land in all weather conditions. With four seasons, bountiful fields with rich grasses, and woods and mountains in the distance, this place offers what I feel they require. They become stronger and more able if need be."

"And Thomas is your helper?"

"Thomas was raised to become the reindeer keeper, as was his father and his father before him. It is the highest honor an elf can be given. He's adapted well. Fitting in is always the plan. He goes unnoticed as he cares for the reindeer. That's why you were chosen."

"I don't understand, Santa."

"When that stranger, as you call him, died, I searched to find someone qualified to take his place."

"Take his place?"

"You may have thought of him as a stranger, but he was Thomas' helper. I chose him to assist Thomas in the ways of the people and to spend time with Thomas and the reindeer. In return, he was given the farmhouse and all the surroundings. He may have been odd to most, but he had the heart of a child, as do you."

Abbey sat, trying to absorb everything being told her.

"Reindeer are able to sense a person's values and kindness toward others. Before the old man passed, I asked him for names of people he'd become aware of that might make the perfect match with the reindeer keeper. Once he gave me names, I went searching."

"Searching?"

Santa reached under the seat and pulled out a rather large satchel. Stepping down off the sleigh, he turned and held out his hand. "I'll explain, Abbey."

It was obvious Thomas knew Santa would be bringing Abbey back inside. In place were two chairs sitting next to the tree, along with a small table holding Santa's pipe and two cups of hot chocolate.

"From the looks of it, Thomas, you've had a wonderful time." Santa smiled. He and Abbey sat down.

"That I have. That I have, Santa."

Thomas and his family had exchanged gifts while feasting on cookies sent from Mrs. Claus. As the elves continued to visit, Santa and Abbey spent time together.

Before he could get a word out, Abbey spoke. "I never met that man, Santa. He judged me by my father."

"That's true, Abbey. But I chose you from these."

Santa opened the satchel lying on the table and pulled out letters held together by a ribbon. "The stranger judged both you and your father by your actions toward others. What children write in their letters to me tells me how they will treat others as adults. Compassion stems from the heart of a child."

Santa undid the ribbon and adjusted his glasses. "You wrote this when you were five."

> *Dear Santa,*
> *Jack is sick. Please bring him lots of toys. Mommy stays at the hospital with Jack. Please bring paint brushes to Mommy. She draws good pictures. I miss Mommy. I miss Jack. Me and Daddy made you cookies. Mommy said I was a good cook. My kittens are really big. Please bring them a new ball. I will leave you milk, too, and sugar for your reindeer. How are your reindeer? Merry Christmas, Santa. Daddy told me the hospital has a chimney.*
> *Love,*
> *Abbey*

As Santa folded the letter and opened the envelope, Abbey caught sight of a big crayon heart with lots of Xs and Os drawn all over it. Abbey remembered sitting with her father at the kitchen table, laughing and eating cookies while decorating the envelope. Crayons and paper were everywhere.

"You wrote this when you were three, Abbey." Santa took a sip from his cup as he opened another letter. "Your mother added a note, telling me she wrote it exactly as you said it. She also said you insisted on drawing reindeer all over it."

> *Dear Santa,*
> *Me and mommy made you cookies. Please bring Jack new skates. Mommy, too. I love you, Santa. I will leave you cookies and sugar for all the reindeers. How is Rudolph's nose? Please bring Daddy candy. Mommy said his tooth is sweet.*
> *Love,*
> *Abbey*

She was in tears. Before Santa could fold the letter, Abbey stopped him. She wanted to see her mother's handwriting. She tried imagining her mother getting Christmas ready, filling the stockings and fixing a snack for Santa. Abbey sensed she herself readied her family as her mother had done. She never felt like this before. Her heart was aching.

"You wrote this when you were nine, Abbey."

As Santa opened the letter, Abbey could see it was written in cursive. Abbey recalled taking her time with every word. She wanted it perfect for Santa.

> *Dear Santa,*
>
> *My friends don't believe in you. I tell them there has to be a Santa Claus because you always listen to me, no matter what I ask you to bring. I heard my mommy crying again. My father told me she doesn't feel very good. We didn't make you cookies so I will leave you a sandwich. I hope that is okay. Can you make my mom feel better? I miss her. We all do. I love you, Santa. Thank you for believing in me.*
>
> *Love,*
> *Abbey*

"I brought one more of your letters, Abbey. You wrote this when you were a month shy of fifteen."

> *Dear Santa,*
>
> *I don't know why I am writing this letter to you because I know you aren't real. This is our first Christmas without Mom. I am all mixed up. Sometimes I miss her, but most times I am mad at her. I know she had problems, but she didn't have to leave us. I think Jack is angry, too, but he never talks about her. He is always with his friends. I try to make my father happy because he misses her so much. If you were real, I would ask that you help my family. I miss being a family.*
>
> *Love,*
> *Abbey*

Putting the letter down, Santa went over to Abbey, who was crying so hard she couldn't breathe. He put his arms around her and hugged her. He handed her a handkerchief.

"Tears heal the heart, Abbey. They let the pain go. When we love somebody so much, sadly, we can hate them just as much if they hurt us. But the trouble with that is every day is precious. Every day is a gift, the kind of gift that matters."

Abbey wiped her eyes while quietly asking, "Why did you bring the letters? Why me, Santa?"

Sitting back down Santa explained. "In all your letters, you never once asked me for anything material for yourself. You always asked for others. I knew you'd grow to be a caring adult, understanding of those around you. That is how I chose you to help the reindeer keeper."

"But I've not been caring when dealing with my own mother."

"If you didn't love her, Abbey, there would be no tears. I have one more letter. A little girl wrote this a very long time ago when she was six."

> Dear Santa,
> This picture is for you. I had fun drawing your reindeer. Mommy and I made you cookies. We made lots of cookies. I gave lots of them away. My sister would like a doll. I think a doll bed would be nice too. My daddy needs new boots, and my brother John would love a new book for his stamps. Mommy likes flowers, so, if you bring her a pretty pot, it would be nice. Thank you, Santa. I love you.
> Abigail

"My mother wrote that, didn't she?"

"Yes, Abbey. You take after her, thinking of others instead of your-self."

"I'm starting to understand, Santa."

"It's not easy to let it go."

"Guess we make the choice of what to remember."

"That we do."

Santa reached inside his satchel and pulled out a small gift wrapped in tissue paper. "This is for you, Abbey."

Abbey was speechless.

"Please, go ahead and open it."

Abbey undid the paper and let it fall to the floor. She hesitated. Her heart was beating. She pulled the top of the white box open and found more tissue. Setting the gift on the table, Abbey moved the paper aside and reached in to find a wooden box with flowers painted all over it.

At first, it was just a wooden box. But then the memory of a little girl with her mother came to mind. A beautiful mother smelling of lilacs was sitting at the kitchen table above a funeral home, watching her daughter paint a present for Santa Claus.

"Santa has to have a present, too, Mommy," the daughter told the mother as she dipped her brush in oranges and yellows and reds and greens.

It was snowing outside. Gifts wrapped and gifts waiting to be wrapped were everywhere. The smell of gingerbread cooking and breads baked and cooling surrounded the two.

Santa spoke. "Open the box, Abbey."

Abbey did as Santa asked. She found an envelope with "For Santa Claus" beautifully written on the back. Abbey knew that writing. It was from her mother. With a lump in her throat, Abbey opened the envelope.

> *Dear Santa,*
> *This box is for you. Each flower was painted by my beautiful, little daughter, Abbey, who felt Santa should have a present, too. Abbey said the flowers are like the ones grown in our garden. Merry Christmas, Santa.*
> *Love,*
> *Abbey and Abigail*

"I believe, Santa," said Abbey between more tears. "I believe, as my mother did."

"I know you do. That is why you were chosen."

"Thank you for this gift. I will cherish it forever."

The reindeer keeper whispered to Santa. It was time to begin his journey.

"You're right, Thomas. I do have a long night ahead of me. Abbey must get some rest. Her family is home for Christmas."

With her mother's letter inside, Abbey wrapped the box back in the tissue paper. She stood. "In my heart, I knew there was a Santa Claus."

"In my heart, Abbey, I knew you were the one."

Santa hugged Abbey. He shook Thomas' hand.

Saying good-bye, Santa walked out of the barn.

Shimmering crystals swirled faster and faster as he boarded the sleigh. Picking up the reins, Santa signaled to his reindeer. Standing in the snow with Thomas by her side, Abbey watched as the sleigh circled above the barn and then disappeared among the stars. That bellowing voice and bells tinkling faded into the night.

"It's magic, Miss Abbey. The spirit of Christmas is magic," said Thomas.

"It truly is, Thomas. Now what will you do? Christmas is here. The reindeer have been chosen."

"But next Christmas is not far away. A reindeer keeper's duties are never done."

Abbey looked around and realized Thomas' family was nowhere to be seen. "Where did they go? I didn't see them in Santa's sleigh."

"Elves don't require a sleigh, Miss Abbey. They were needed at the North Pole."

"You have a lovely family, Thomas."

"And so do you, Miss Abbey. You best be going back. They will soon be up for Christmas morning."

"Will you come for breakfast?"

"I thank you but I do have my work to do. There will be time for many breakfasts together, Miss Abbey. A Merry, Merry Christmas to you."

"And a Merry Christmas to you, reindeer keeper."

"Wait until Steve sees how much snow has fallen," thought Abbey as she walked back home.

It wasn't until she was inside that she realized she hadn't worn a coat or boots. Looking at the clock, she was astonished to find it hadn't budged. Being with Santa seemed to have made time stand still. Abbey picked up the photo of her parents she'd left lying on the sofa and placed it back on the shelf. Next to it, she put the wooden box. She locked the back door, went upstairs, and fell sound asleep.

Chapter Nine

STEVE CHECKED THE WEATHER CONDITIONS OUT the back window. It was what he did every morning-even Christmas morning. With the snow letting up, the distant mountains seemed to be wrapped in a fleece blanket.

"It looks like one of your paintings, Abbey. Reminds me of those Christmases when the boys were little and we'd take your father with us to your grandparents. This place is starting to feel like home."

"As soon as Eric told me he felt he was home, I knew we were."

Getting more eggs out of the refrigerator, Abbey kept talking. "I had the strangest dream last night. Thomas was in it. Everything was so vivid."

"Thomas does leave a lot to the imagination," remarked Sam as he came into the kitchen. "I just saw him drive in. Does he work every day?

"Barn work doesn't take a holiday. Merry Christmas, Sammy," said Steve.

"Merry Christmas, Dad." Hugging Abbey and wishing her a Merry Christmas, Sam continued, "Too bad we don't have more time. Cate is enjoying herself. She's never been around snow. She's never had a real Christmas tree."

"Maybe you can come back during the summer," suggested Abbey. "It always was your favorite time of the year."

As Sam finished explaining his hectic schedule, Eric joined them. Even though he was up, he still looked half-asleep.

62

"Merry Christmas, son." Steve stood and shook Eric's hand.

"Merry Christmas, everyone. What's cooking?"

"Getting ready to make more cinnamon rolls," said Abbey.

"Need some help?"

"You can do the pancakes and French toast when everyone is ready."

"Great, Mom. I haven't had a pancake in years." Turning to Sam, Eric continued. "Meg will be right down. She had the best run yesterday. It must be the fresh air because she wants to go again this morning."

"Thermometer says it's only five above," Steve laughed.

As Abbey cracked the eggs, an image of her outside in the cold without boots or a coat popped into her head. She dismissed it when Meg and Cate came into the kitchen.

"So when do we open presents?" asked Sam.

"After breakfast. Like always." Abbey reminded him.

"Looks like Santa was here. The stockings are full," added Eric.

"I never had a Christmas stocking." Meg put her mittens on.

"You must have!" said Abbey.

"Not that I remember. Once they divorced, Christmas never mattered."

Abbey read between the lines, sensing lingering grief despite the high profile.

"We won't be long, Mom. If possible, I'd like to get to the cemetery. There'll be no time in the morning."

"I'd like to go, too," added Eric.

"We should have time before dinner. Don't think you have to go. Your grandparents would understand."

No one said a thing as Abbey referenced her mother. She never referenced her mother in any way.

"Sounds like a plan. See you shortly." Sam and Meg disappeared into the cold.

Breakfast came together like one of Sam's well-worked scripts. Even Meg complimented Eric, suggesting he take some of his cookbooks back with them. After the kitchen was in order, attention focused on opening gifts. Steve turned the tree lights on while Abbey lit the candles.

The boys tackled their stockings as if they were back in preschool.

Abbey didn't just put things inside; she wrapped every little item. Cate loved it all: socks, soaps, some small photo albums, and stuff for her camera. Abbey had called Eric for suggestions concerning Meg's. That's why her stocking included running socks and tights. Eric had told Abbey about a lavender lotion and a certain brand of granola bars. Both young women received the granola bars and a favorite print of Abbey's of Eric and Sam from a Christmas long ago.

Abbey's gift overwhelmed Steve. He'd forgotten about the photo. He tried explaining the particular joke they were laughing at, but it didn't sound as funny as when Abbey's father told it. Ironically, Steve had done the same for Abbey. He'd taken favorite pictures of her father and made them into a book. Photos were placed in chronological order with dates and intimate notes included. Of course, he bought her flavored coffees, lotions, and gift certificates to her favorite shops, but the book was the gift that left everyone in tears.

Even though there weren't little ones in the house, there were lots of presents. The boys made sure their parents had a wonderful Christmas. Abbey told them they didn't need a thing, that their coming home would be enough. But they didn't listen. Eric and Sam bought them tickets to London. From there, they'd be able to travel Europe via the train. It was something they always talked about doing.

"It's during the summer, Mom," explained Eric. "You can stay with us overnight. We'll take you to the airport and pick you up."

"We thought that'd be a good time to go. You'll be out of school. No problem with leaving the lumberyard."

Before Steve could say a thing, Abbey was on her feet and hugging them both. "No problem at all. Thank you so much. What a beautiful gift. It's a dream come true."

Steve put on a similar act. No one had a clue there just might be a problem at the lumberyard.

It seemed as if it took forever to open presents. One was saved for last.

"This is why I went into town yesterday." Meg handed Abbey a beautifully wrapped gift.

"You didn't have to, Meg."

"I wanted to. I remembered something Eric once told me after we arrived."

All eyes were on Abbey as she pulled the curly ribbon off the rather large present.

"I feel like a little kid." Abbey laughed. "I'm the one who is supposed to be surprising everyone."

"Just rip it open, Mom," said Sam.

"You know me. I like to save the paper."

Abbey finally opened the box. Pulling back layers of bubble wrap, her face turned white. It wasn't what was inside that startled her. Thoughts of last night's dream came rushing at her again—the sleigh, the elves, and Santa talking to Abbey as if he was real—as if those reindeer right outside the window were truly his reindeer.

"How silly," she told herself for even contemplating Santa Claus was real.

Abbey reached inside and pulled out brushes, acrylics, canvas, and oils—anything anyone could wish for if inclined to dabble in art.

"Eric once told me you are an artist like your mother. He said you use oils to create just as she did," Meg explained. "Yesterday I stood outside where flowers blooming and leaves changing filled my mind. I saw the way the front porch winds around to the back, and I envisioned you putting it all on canvas. I hope you don't think I'm being presumptuous, but something led me to that art store."

No one spoke. No one knew what to say. No one ever discussed her mother. Abbey felt overwhelmed, not by those watching her but by the gnawing feeling that if she looked up on that shelf set back on the wall, she might see something she thought was part of a dream.

"Dare I? Dare I even think that what I've dismissed as a dream was actually real?" Abbey struggled to make sense of what she was consuming her. "Dare I, an adult with worries, sorrows, and flaws bigger than the Grand Canyon believe as the children do? Could I believe as purely as they do that there really is a Santa Claus? Really and truly a Santa Claus?"

Abbey put the art materials back inside and closed the box. She took a deep breath. Slowly turning toward the tree, she tilted her head up to see beyond the branches. There it was. Next to a picture of a handsome couple on their wedding day, there was that wooden box with painted flowers, a box full of beautiful memories of a mother smelling like lilacs sitting by her daughter in the spirit of giving to the one who gives to so many on Christmas.

"I didn't mean to upset you." Meg was in tears, thinking Abbey was offended. "I don't know what I was thinking. I am not part of your family or any family."

It was all coming out on this Christmas morning in the farmhouse.

"Eric, I've been so cold. I'm so sorry. I couldn't bear it if you left me too. I'm sorry, everyone. I didn't mean to ruin today." In tears, Meg was about to run out of the room.

Now Abbey did the talking. "You are part of this family, Meg. My mother was an artist, a beautiful artist. I used to paint with my mother when I was a little girl. I vaguely remember, but I do remember." Abbey stopped for a moment. She looked at the wooden box. "When she died, I felt she'd abandoned me. I would have nothing to do with anything that resembled her in any way. I'm trying to own the hatred I've kept inside. It's not easy. If you accept the anger and disappointment at your age, Meg, you won't spend the rest of your life despising your mother. You didn't walk in her shoes. I know that doesn't lessen the pain, but you don't know what she was going through. Let it go, Meg. Let life in." Now by her side, Abbey continued, "I love your gift. It was very thoughtful. Ever since we moved into this beautiful home, I've been thinking it's time to paint again."

"Don't go, Meg. You have a family who loves you." Eric took his wife into his arms and held her.

All that could be heard was the rustling of paper as the others picked up around them.

Abbey whispered to Sam and Cate, "They need some time alone. It's probably the most they've talked in a long time." A knock at the back door caught Abbey's attention.

Already in the kitchen, Steve opened the door. "Merry Christmas, Thomas. Come in."

"The Merriest Christmas to you, Mr. Steve."

"I'm glad you stopped." Abbey hugged Thomas.

"'Tis a magical time for sure, Miss Abbey."

"Can you stay?"

"Thank you again, but there's much to be done. This is for you, Miss Abbey."

Thomas placed the ribbon Santa had used to hold those letters to-gether in Abbey's hand. "I must go." He looked at Abbey in a way only she could understand.

"Good-bye, everyone." He left as quietly as he came.

Abbey swore she saw those crystals follow him out the door and down the steps.

"A ribbon? Why would he stop to give you a ribbon?" asked Steve.

"To Thomas, it's a special ribbon. Now it's my special ribbon." She put it in her pocket and poured herself some coffee. "When Eric and Meg are ready, we can take a quick trip to the cemetery if you still want to?"

"Definitely, Mom," said Sam. "Do you mind if Cate and I take one last skate around the pond?"

"Please go. Enjoy yourselves."

About an hour or so later, they were all back in the kitchen. Eric and Meg seemed to have gotten rid of a huge weight off their shoulders. With the prime rib cooking, they piled into Eric's Tahoe and headed to the cemetery.

Chapter Ten

TALK OF COOKBOOKS AND PHOTOGRAPHS, FAR-OFF places, and letting go made the ride pass by without notice. Since it was a holiday, the plows hadn't cleared a pathway in so Eric pulled off on the shoulder as far as he could.

"Do you think it's acceptable that I take photographs?" asked Cate.

"My father always said death is a part of life," explained Abbey.

Because there was even more snow than before, Abbey had to get her bearings. Spotting the maple tree, Abbey led the way. The backdrop was striking. With headstones dating back to the 1700s, it felt like a walk through history books. Creating little swirls of white, the wind made it feel even colder than it was.

"Look at those monuments." Sam pointed. "They dwarf the rest."

"They must be of prominence," said Steve.

"Or some wishing they were. I'm seeing all of this through the lens. Reading a headstone only gives you the beginning and the end. What about the in-between stuff?"

"That's why I enjoy reading obituaries." Abbey continued through the cemetery.

"When you think about it, going to a cemetery on Christmas makes perfect sense. It's visiting family," said Eric.

"Well put." Sam stopped to read a headstone.

"I hear bells." Cate was searching all around her.

"Behind you, honey."

They all turned in time to see two horses pulling a sleigh. As it approached, they could see a family out for a Christmas afternoon excursion. Scarves flying seemed to be waving at this other family standing between tombstones. The horses picked up speed. They were quickly out of sight.

"Over here!" Abbey shouted.

"This is a perfect spot. We all know how Grandpa loved trees. The view takes in the valley where he'd pick apples in the fall." Sam cleared away some of the snow with his boot. He held Abbey's arm as he knelt down beside her.

"It's so peaceful. Besides the train, all you can hear is the wind through the pine trees." Eric was on the other side of his mother.

Without anyone noticing, Cate took some shots of them from behind, at a distance in black and white. Steve stood off to the side. Meg remained silent behind Eric.

"You must miss him, Mom. I only wish I'd spent more time with him," said Sam.

"That's a normal feeling when someone we care for dies. What matters is he knew you loved him."

"I'm glad he didn't suffer."

"Ironically, he passed in his sleep, as did my mother."

"Both in their sleep," Eric asked. "What did your mother die from?"

Abbey freed her hand of a woolen mitten. She cleaned the snow away from her father's name—and this time her mother's name which they shared. Abbey understood it was at her father's urging she be given the name. After such a difficult birth, Abbey's mother was overjoyed with her beautiful daughter. She'd feared the worst with each wrenching pain.

"She died from diabetes. She was much too young, but then death is not in our hands."

Curious, Sam asked, "What does her middle initial stand for?"

Abbey outlined the "G" with her finger. "That is for a movie actress both my grandparents idolized. I'm thankful I wasn't given my mother's full name."

"So what is it?"

"It's Greta, Sam. Abigail Greta!"

"I love it! Sammy and I already have names picked out for our kids."

Without questioning the fact they weren't married and realizing any rules she'd been brought up with had long since disappeared, Abbey replied, "When you do have children, Cate, it'd be best if you were settled. Children need roots."

"True, Mom," replied Sam. "We've talked about that. But it's such a connected world now. They also need to know their global neighbors. That's how understanding begins."

"It's changed since your mother and I raised the both of you. Years back, you could go to work and never have to worry about your job. Nothing is secure now. We're thankful the four of you have your feet firmly planted. But keep in mind that it's wise to have a game plan."

"You're both secure, aren't you? You've worked so hard to give us what we needed and more," said Eric.

"Back when we started out, it was much simpler. My guidance counselor told me I could be a nurse or a teacher. That was it. I've been teaching for over thirty years."

"Ever think about retiring?" Eric asked.

"I hadn't until we moved into the farmhouse." Abbey's thoughts turned to the barn and those reindeer.

"What about you, Dad? Guess it's different since you own the lumberyard. Would you sell? Is there someone who'd be interested in buying it?" asked Eric.

Steve couldn't find the words to answer Eric's question.

Abbey broke the silence. "All options are on the table."

Sam detected a problem. After all, recording people was his passion. "What is it, Dad? I've never seen that look on your face."

Despite the fact that he and Abbey had decided not to mention the big-box store coming in, Steve found he had no control of the words that filled that solemn field.

"Why didn't you tell us?"

"We didn't want to worry you, Sam. You all have enough on your shoulders."

Meg spoke up. "My firm is not secure. No matter how many hours I put in or how hard I work, I could go in any day and find they no longer need me. As you always say, Abbey, things happen for reasons."

"What do you mean Meg?" asked Eric.

"I'm not sure. Being away from it all for only a few days has made me look at our life together differently. I never realized how much you loved cooking. You are so alive in that kitchen. It's the Eric I fell in love with." A rabbit scurrying about the monuments broke the seriousness of the moment. "I'm going to try to not let my anger control me. If and when I get past it, I hope I'll find a mother who loves me."

Now standing, Eric wrapped Meg up in his arms as Steve helped Abbey to her feet. They circled the headstone and joined hands in prayer.

"We better get back. The roast should be about done." Abbey held Meg back as the others walked ahead.

"I myself am realizing that a daughter can be a mother's toughest critic. I'll be with you every step of the way."

"I feel your strength, Abbey."

"I sense your determination Meg. I'm very proud of you."

"Look! More rabbits." Cate had her camera shooting one frame after another.

"When you do have children, Cate," noted Abbey as she and Meg caught up with everyone, "they will have a mother full of life and wonder."

"I only have one question," remarked Steve. "Who'll be doing the night shift?"

"As you said yourself, Dad, it's a totally different world. I'll be pulling night duty as much as Cate."

"As it should be." Cate smiled.

No one realized it had even snowed. Eric went ahead, cleaned off the windshield, and turned on the heat. They kept talking all the way back to the farmhouse.

Chapter Eleven

ABBEY HAD PLANNED ON EATING AT about four. She figured that would give everyone time to prepare for their early-morning departure. Sam and Cate couldn't risk missing their flight. They had reservations for Brazil the next day. Eric kicked right in, making the gravy and doctoring the mashed potatoes. Cate took pictures as he lifted the roast out of the oven.

"Which ones do you want to bring back with us, Eric?" Meg was going through his old cookbooks. Some had scribbles on the pages. His favorite recipes had stars around them.

"I can't choose, honey."

"Then if you don't mind, Abbey, we'll take them all."

"They are Eric's to do with as he pleases."

"That one with all the cookies on the cover belongs with you, Mom," said Eric. "It must have been one of Grandma's favorites. She marked just about every recipe. She even added her own versions. I remember thinking her recipes sounded better than the ones in the book."

"I'll keep it with the others." Abbey leafed through its pages. Seeing that writing again brought her back to those letters. She looked out the window and saw the stars sparkling above the barn. It had truly been a Christmas to remember.

Before anyone sat down at the table set with dishes used for generations, Cate took pictures. The centerpiece was made from branches

Thomas had trimmed from the Christmas tree. Candles illuminated the dining room. When ready, Eric placed the prime rib in front of his father. With everyone seated and a prayer said, Steve took the lead, slicing the roast as Abbey's dad had done before him. Serving bowls were passed. Salads were heaped into side dishes. Rolls and breads were buttered. Conversation flowed, as did the wine. Just as the table was being cleared for cheesecake drizzled in blueberries, the phone rang. It was Jack. After wishing everyone a Merry Christmas, he and Abbey talked.

"Well"?

"I know what you're asking, Abbey. The answer is yes. We took our vows standing barefoot on the beach. Nothing fancy. We were dressed in shorts and drenched in sun screen. I've learned it doesn't matter what you wear. It's a gamble any way you do it."

"Give your bride our congratulations. We look forward to meeting her."

"I'd put her on the phone, but she's disappeared. Tell you the truth, it doesn't feel like Christmas. I remember our Christmases, Abbey, the ones before Mom died."

"It's time we remember all of them, Jack. They're all part of who we are."

With tentative plans to meet in the city, Jack went back to the beach while Abbey went back to the table with a small gift for each one of them.

"What's this? More presents?" asked Steve.

"Just a little something unexpected. Christmas shouldn't be so predictable."

"Couldn't have said it better myself," remarked Sam.

"Dig in and open up." Abbey laughed. She watched her family unwrap the treasures she'd found at the dollar store.

They lingered over coffee and dessert until there wasn't a blueberry or slice of cake left. After the dishes were cleaned and put away, they spent time around the tree. With a fire in the fireplace and wine glasses tingling, Eric made a toast.

"Our hours together may have been few but we made the best of every minute. Same time next year, everyone."

"To the promise of tomorrow," Sam added.

After they'd gone to bed, Abbey put the ribbon Thomas had given her inside the wooden box next to her mother's letter.

"Right where it belongs," she told herself.

Chapter Twelve

IT WAS THE END OF MARCH. In some places, snow was still on the ground.

Since Christmas, retiring had become more than a vague concept. Abbey had always considered such a move as fading away from life. But now with the farmhouse, her rekindled interest in painting, and, of course, her responsibilities to Santa Claus, retirement was the next phase she was ready to begin. She'd given her notice at school. She and Steve had talked to their financial adviser. Abbey's last day would be June 26.

So much for best laid plans. The call came just as she was introducing the letter *R* to her class. Abbey asked the secretary to take a message, but the caller insisted on speaking with her. Two minutes later, her life was plummeting out of control. She tried not to let it show as she left the principal's office. She tried not to run out the door screaming that results from tests done a few weeks earlier were crushing.

As Abbey drew upper- and lowercase *Rs*, the reality of that cancer back, eating her up at a rapid rate, about froze her in fear. As her students tried to replicate the letter, thoughts of how she would break it to Steve flashed through her mind. They'd been together for as long as she could remember. How could she tell him that everything they'd worked for might never be realized? They'd faced obstacles before. From the tone spoken over the phone, this could be her last challenge.

"One good thing," she thought as she helped her class pick up for snack time. "The big-box store's opening has been delayed."

A task force had been formed. Citizens were attempting to keep it out, but she and Steve were realistic. They knew it would open. Abbey decided she'd tell Steve in the quiet of dinnertime. She had to be at the doctor's in the morning.

But when she arrived home, the phone was ringing.

"Oh, Eric. Hello. Nothing's wrong. I'm just getting in. What's going on? You never call this time of day."

"It's Meg. She's been let go, Mom. She doesn't know what she'll do."

Again Abbey understood what Meg was feeling. But she didn't burden her son with her own devastating news. She had to grasp hold of it before comforting those around her.

"Meg is talented, Eric. She's strong and well respected in her field. I've always told you things happen for reasons."

"I know Mom. It's just the not knowing what's next."

As her eldest son kept talking, tears flowed down Abbey's cheeks. Images of her rocking him in the middle of the night flashed through her mind. She could smell the talcum powder and hear his little sighs as he slept in her arms. She had to get off the phone.

"Someone is at the front door, Eric. Let me talk to your father tonight. I'll call you tomorrow. I know it is easy for me to say, but don't worry. You will get through this. Give my love to Meg."

DINNER CONVERSATION CENTERED ON MEG AND Eric. Abbey decided she'd go alone to the appointment, absorb the news, and then offer Steve some hope, even if there might not be any.

Hours later, lying next to the man she'd surrendered to at age sixteen in the back of a Chevy truck, Abbey remained content with her decision. Steve had enough on his mind. With his back to her and the wind howling, Abbey put her arm around him, as she often did while he slept. His warmth and the faint scent of wood mingled with varnish and aftershave from morning were security to Abbey. He'd always been her rock. He rarely became unglued. Abbey caressed the nape of his neck and moved closer. She felt insulated from the evil attacking her body.

Instead of projecting, she looked back to that evening when she'd told her dad she and Steve were going to the drive-in. It wasn't a lie.

81

They did go. They just never saw the movie. That had been the first time. There were many more. He was the most handsome boy she'd ever seen. Remembering how he walked right by the popular senior girls at a school dance to ask her to dance made her heart beat faster even now.

"He knew my name," she reflected. "He knew my name. When we danced, I felt as if I'd known him forever."

She couldn't stop the tears. Lying there, wrapped in his strength, she felt possibility. Abbey had been the envy of all her friends. Steve was captain of the football team and head of the debate team. He loved a good argument backed with facts. To say Steve was the love of her life was inadequate.

"So yes," she thought. "It'd be best if I went alone. It will be my turn to cradle Steve."

Abbey started the next day as she did any other, going to the barn and then to school. She informed her principal she needed a half-day. She told Steve she might be late. This wasn't uncommon.

Abbey was early for her appointment.

After the initial check-in, the nurse told Abbey to take a seat. "The doctor is running behind," she explained.

"Why do doctors do this?" Abbey wondered. "Don't they know just getting to an appointment takes every bit of strength one has? Every minute waiting is an eternity."

In the end, Abbey wished the doctor had kept her waiting. She was told the cancer was aggressive and spreading throughout her body. Abbey was given options and told what to expect. She didn't care about losing her hair or throwing up so violently that it would leave her weak on the bathroom floor. It was her family. That was her concern. No matter how old they'd become, the boys were still her babies.

Driving home in a sudden spring blizzard, tears were falling as fast as the snowflakes. She'd encourage Steve to find someone. The thought of him being alone frightened her. She'd intensify her hints to Sam about marrying and settling down.

"Life is hard enough for a child without a place to call home," she reasoned with herself.

She had no doubt he and Cate would be good parents, but it'd be easier to do with roots firmly cemented. As far as Eric and Meg, Abbey felt it was time for them to come home. They could move into the farmhouse. The place was certainly big enough. Area law firms would fight over Meg. A four-year college renowned for its culinary courses was only fifty minutes away. With transfer credits, Eric could move right along. In the meantime, he could help Steve prepare for the competition. Eric had great friends running cutting-edge marketing firms. He could get their input. That was the plan for the rest of their lives, according to Abbey.

Turning into the driveway, her thoughts focused on Meg. Having her with them would be like having the daughter they'd lost.

About an hour or so after dinner, Abbey told Steve in the quiet of their living room. He sobbed uncontrollably, falling to his knees on the old plank floor. Gathering him in her arms, Abbey stayed beside him. When she felt Steve was strong enough, she stood and led him to the sofa, where they stayed until the wee hours, talking and remembering. As the north wind shifted the snow from one drift to another, the moon made its way to that wooden box painted in flowers.

Chapter Thirteen

NOW OFFICIALLY ON LEAVE, ABBEY WAS in the midst of tests and pre-liminary work. A treatment plan of chemo and most likely radiation would follow. Steve was trying to stay upbeat, but Abbey knew he broke down when he was alone. The boys called most every day. Sam was still in Brazil. Meg called constantly. Abbey sensed the fear in her voice. Meg had started letting go of old feelings. She'd started trusting again. Abbey couldn't leave her now. She knew only too well how much that hurt.

Eric and Meg were coming around to Abbey's way of thinking. Since going back after Christmas, Meg confided in Abbey that Eric was find-ing it harder to keep up the pace. His heart was in a kitchen, any kitchen. Shortly after that, Abbey told Meg about the nearby college and con-nections she had with law firms. The next day Meg called to say they were coming home. When Abbey told Steve of their plans, his relief was visible.

"So that means we won't be alone?" Steve asked as they watched the sun rise one morning.

"You could say that, honey."

"Five o'clock. I'll pick you up. Be ready."

"Where are we going?"

"My secret."

"Remember, we don't keep secrets."

"Then call it a surprise."

Getting her mind off the cancer was a welcome change. "It's such a dirty word. They should call it something more uplifting," Abbey told herself while waiting for Steve. "But nothing could sugarcoat such a monster. Call it whatever you want, it still means the same."

It felt good to wonder what Steve was up to. That one word hadn't defined her day. Instead, she found herself putting on some makeup and caring about what she wore.

Steve walked through the door right on time. "Leave the worries here. We're going on a date."

Abbey assumed he'd be taking her to their restaurant; maybe he would have flowers and a violinist. But not so. Steve headed in the opposite direction. Abbey worried he'd lost it when he turned into an empty field and put the truck in four-wheel drive.

"We can't go onto someone's land. Are you sure you know where you're going?"

"We'll be there in a minute. Let me get my bearings."

Steve rolled down the window, took a second to look out, and then turned the truck around. He moved ahead a few feet and then shut the engine off. "From my calculations, this would be about it."

"Be what?"

"This would be where I robbed you of your virginity, you little rascal you!"

It didn't register at first. With her mind full of adult worries, going back to a time of sock hops and Friday night football was a stretch. But then it hit. Steve was taking her on a date back to where they began. She rolled down the window and tried to remember where the screen had been located. She tried to picture where the cinder block building with restrooms and concession had stood. Abbey shut her eyes and breathed in the night air in hopes of smelling hotdogs smothered in onions and greasy fries.

"I couldn't have asked for anything more. This is better than any restaurant or show."

"Oh, but the show is just getting underway."

Steve reached back and pulled up an oversized shopping bag. He stepped out of the truck and replaced his vest with something from inside the bag. "The old jacket doesn't fit like it used to but I'm still your number sixty-five, first-string varsity quarterback."

Abbey had worn the jacket every day once they started going steady. She'd sewn each emblem and patch in place. Although frayed, they were still intact.

"Where did you find it?"

"When we moved, I found a trunk of oldies but goodies."

Out came movie stubs and letters they'd written each other when he was in Vietnam.

"You were the reason I made it home, Abbey."

Out from that bag came more memories, a wedding invitation and birth announcements with teddy bears dressed in blue. Memory after memory came out of that bag.

"Close your eyes."

Abbey dared not peek. It was obvious Steve had planned every detail. The second he put something in her hand, she knew what it was. She'd worn his class ring around her neck through her senior year. All her friends were jealous. Upperclassmen hardly ever dated anyone below them. When they did, it was for one thing only. Steve and Abbey proved that myth false.

"I thought it was lost. This ring was a part of me for what seemed forever back then."

"You are my forever, Abbey."

Steve stepped outside again and turned back around. In the same tone and with the same awestruck look of years past, he asked, "Would you like to dance, Abbey?"

Before she could question, his hand was waiting for hers. There was no hesitating. No words were spoken. From the back of the truck came his old battery-operated radio. He pushed a button; then escorted Abbey to the middle of the field. There were still no words. None were needed. Steve took Abbey into his arms. Kissing the tip of her nose, Steve pulled her close, leading her one step at a time.

"It's our song, Steve," Abbey whispered. She melted into his arms as the snowflakes kept falling.

With the moon as their spotlight, the couple moved ever so slowly. Though years had gone by, their love had only deepened. Throughout all they'd endured, they remained one. Now more than ever, that's what they were determined to do.

As the lyrics floated towards the mountains, Steve whispered, "Take my hand, Abbey. Take my whole life, too, for I couldn't help falling in love with you."

Around and around they swirled. Through the crisp night air echoed the distant howl of a passing train. Its melancholy tone did not dampen the moment. Rather it only heightened emotions. Stopping, Steve outlined her lips with his fingertips. He pulled Abbey even closer and kissed her with a passion as strong and wild as it had been so many years ago at this very spot.

"As our song keeps telling us, some things are meant to be. We were meant to be, Abbey." He picked her up in his arms.

That passion led them once again into the backseat of a Chevy truck. Rapturously and with even more meaning than that first time, they made love. With Gene Pitney telling of that "Town Without Pity," as Roy Orbison belted out "Crying," and as the Righteous Brothers swooned in their "Unchained Melody," the two lovers rocked the night away.

Chapter Fourteen

THE SNOW HAD FINALLY MELTED INTO spring without notice. Just as amazing were April's early flowers blooming all around the farmhouse. Tulips lined the driveway. Some spread about the many rock gardens, mingling with lilies of the valley just waking up.

Tests were complete. Abbey was about to start treatment. Having been told how sick she might get, she decided to bring out the oils and canvas. On sunny days, she'd sit amongst the gardens and paint. On rainy days, she'd sit on the back porch.

Her list of things to do was long. Included was making way for Eric and Meg. So much had happened. They found a buyer for their Manhattan brownstone quicker than they'd anticipated. Eric had given his notice. He was busy wrapping up with his clients. Abbey sensed a relief in his voice as leaving the rat race was becoming a reality. Equally relieved was Steve. Having Eric with him at the lumberyard would be an unexpected plus. Meg had contacted the school. Eric planned on talking with them once they were back.

There were so many loose ends. Abbey wanted to make sure she had it all covered for her family. She'd heard horror stories from many who'd gone through what she was about to face. At her last doctor's visit, she asked for the truth. She was told the chances of her beating this were slim. She didn't tell Steve. He was worried enough about her.

After painting one morning, Abbey walked to the barn. She visited Thomas every day, but today she went with a distinct purpose. She felt obligated to let Santa know of her situation. She wanted to get a message to him.

Without getting into details, Abbey said, "It's important I contact Santa, Thomas."

"I understand, Miss Abbey."

"Should I write him a letter?"

"No. Let me finish feeding the reindeer. Wait here, Miss Abbey." He was back a few minutes later. "I must ask again, Miss Abbey. Do you believe?"

"With my heart and soul, I believe, Thomas."

Speaking not another word, Thomas took hold of Abbey's hands. "Shut your eyes, Miss Abbey."

Abbey did as Thomas directed. A sudden gush of wind circled them. "Hold on, Miss Abbey."

She felt so light on her feet, as if the wind was carrying her along.

In a matter of seconds, Thomas said, "You may open your eyes, Miss Abbey."

Before she had time to think, fellow elves surrounded Thomas. Mounds of snow were everywhere. Abbey wasn't cold. It took no explaining. This was the North Pole.

With elves talking and giggling, Thomas led Abbey down a cobblestone path. As they walked, Abbey tried to absorb her surroundings.

"This really is the North Pole," she thought. "Not a tourist attraction full of screaming children in the summertime. This is where Santa Claus lives and works."

It reminded Abbey of an out-of-the-way village she and Steve happened upon when travelling through New England back before the boys were born. Rather quaint, it was full of little oddities and buildings of brick and ornate design. The North Pole's hustle and bustle was contagious. What seemed to be a central square was blessed with towering pines.

Thomas explained, "Those smaller homes in the distance are where my fellow elves live." He turned a corner and pointed to the stable. "Would you like to stop and see the reindeer, Miss Abbey? These are Santa's Christmas Eve reindeer ... for now at least."

Abbey knew what that meant. "Definitely," she replied.

The stable made their barn seem small.

"Just because it's not that time of the year doesn't mean there is not work to be done. As I've told you before, it takes all year to get ready." Thomas opened the door. "These reindeer are cared for in the same manner as the ones I tend to."

Thomas guided Abbey around the reindeer. Some were eating, and some were resting. A few were outside. Over the stalls were names known worldwide. Abbey stopped for the longest time in front of Dancer, her favorite reindeer. She once drew Dancer while sitting at her desk in her bedroom over the funeral home. A few times, she asked Santa to make sure Dancer got enough sugar. Now standing in front of the deer, she realized why she preferred this particular reindeer. Abbey had taken dance lessons for a while, but quit after her mother died. Abbey wondered how far she would have gone if she hadn't turned her back on anything to do with her mother.

One very famous reindeer was being brushed.

"Would you like to give Rudolph a brush, Miss Abbey?"

"Me? Brush Rudolph?"

"He loves to be brushed. This is the one reindeer that never changes. There is only one Rudolph."

If it wasn't for that wooden box with the flowers, Abbey would not have believed where she was at this very moment. And as if brushing Rudolph wasn't enough, Thomas then took Abbey to the North Pole's bustling kitchen. It was quite the undertaking coordinating the holiday baking. Recipes old and new were tested. Today, it was the basic chocolate chip cookie.

The minute they were inside, Abbey thought of Eric. The biggest ovens imaginable were lined up along one entire wall. Elves were using paddles to take the cookies out. In the center of the room were long tables, each piled high with bowls, mixers, and ingredients in cans and jars. Refrigerators lined the opposite wall. It took no introduction. Abbey knew the woman at the center of the baking was Mrs. Claus. She was more beautiful than anyone had ever painted and just as gracious.

"Welcome, Abbey. I'm very happy to meet you. I remember reading your letters."

Out of all the letters and after all those years, Abbey was amazed Mrs. Claus remembered hers.

"I especially liked hearing about your kittens. You'll see many kittens here at the North Pole."

Abbey hadn't thought of her kittens in ages. Her mother had been allergic to them but welcomed each one. A man who helped her father had run over her favorite kitten when backing up the hearse. Abbey remembered sobbing in her mother's arms. Afterwards, they found a spot behind the funeral home and buried it. Her mom tied two sticks together and made a cross. The next day, they planted flowers all around the makeshift grave.

"I just took some chocolate chip cookies out of the oven. Would you like some?"

"They're my favorite, Mrs. Claus. Thank you very much."

"Don't let Santa see them. They're his favorite, too."

Mrs. Claus hugged Abbey; then handed her a small bag full of cookies. "Thank you for helping the reindeer keeper. That's a very important responsibility."

"I'm honored Santa chose me," replied Abbey.

"But who will take my place?" she thought.

Back outside, they continued walking down one pathway and then another until Thomas stopped in front of what Abbey knew was the toy factory. A sign in the window stated Santa was in. Opening the door, Thomas waited. He let Abbey go first. Any child would surely have been spellbound by what was in front of her. Without question, children accept this man and his ability to fly around the world on one particular night in a sleigh full of toys pulled by magical reindeer, going down chimneys and eating cookies at every stop.

"Somewhere on the road to adulthood, the wonder of it all dissipates," thought Abbey. "Adults have enough worry on their shoulders. They need a Santa Claus."

Elves painting rocking horses, sewing teddy bears, and testing trains and bicycles mesmerized Abbey. She again realized this was where the letters came and where the lists were made. This was where one rather large man with a burly beard nurtured childhood wonderment.

He now engulfed her in a welcoming embrace. That was all Abbey needed. She couldn't stop the tears. She cried so hard that she couldn't catch her breath. Just as Santa could decipher what children were telling him in their letters, he was able to sense Abbey's tears were not joyful tears.

"We'll be back shortly, Thomas."

Santa led Abbey to his office and shut the door. He handed her a handkerchief and pulled a chair up next to his. They sat down but said nothing. After a few minutes, Abbey told Santa the reason for her visit. She told him everything.

"Eric and Meg are coming home, which means Steve won't be alone. I couldn't bear it if he was alone. I pray Sam and Cate settle down. They talk of having a child." Abbey wiped away more tears. "I'll never be able to hold my grandchildren. I've saved so many things for them, Santa. But they'll never know me. They'll never know how much their grandmother would have loved them. And my boys ... they're my babies, Santa." Abbey hesitated. "And Santa, I wish my mother was here. Oh, Santa, I wish I could go back and tell her I realize she didn't abandon me. I want her to know how sorry I am. Most of all I want to tell her how much I love her."

Abbey was in tears again. She'd been so concerned about everyone else that she hadn't dealt with her own feelings. Santa moved strands of hair out of Abbey's eyes and then held both her hands.

"Abbey, listen carefully. I chose you without having met you. I chose you because deeds you'd done preceded our meeting. You will be leaving a lifetime of kindness to those you love and generations to come. You'll be in their hearts. You won't miss a birthday or a Christmas."

"I wasn't kind in regard to my mother. I loathed even the thought of her. I made it uncomfortable for my family to speak of her in my presence. Such actions do not speak of a kind person."

"Perfection is not a human trait. You're coming to grips with your anger and hurt. Some people never do."

"But my father died thinking I hated my mother."

"Down deep, Abbey, he knew you loved her."

"I am afraid, Santa."

"We're always afraid of the unknown. Do not be afraid, Abbey. Live each day to the fullest. Some people die without living. Live, Abbey. Embrace the day. None of us know what awaits us tomorrow."

"You chose me to guide your reindeer keeper, and I'm letting you down."

"I told you that when the time came, I'd leave it up to you to suggest who should follow."

"I've tried to think of someone, Santa."

Santa pushed his chair back and stood. "Follow me, Abbey."

He opened another door and led Abbey into a narrow room with rows upon rows of shelves stocked with boxes. Each box seemed to be coded by numbers.

"Let me think." He scratched his beard, and then grabbed one box in particular.

Santa walked over to a table and opened it. From what Abbey could tell, the box was full of envelopes. Santa thumbed through and grabbed a certain one. He returned the box to the shelf. Leading Abbey back to his office, Santa sat in his chair and opened the envelope. He took out a few folded sheets of paper.

"I read between the lines, Abbey. Sometimes, the obvious isn't." He put on his glasses.

> *Dear Santa,*
>
> *Please make my mother and daddy happy again. I miss being together. I wish you could make us a family. My brother would like a robot, some matchbox cars, and a new football. His football is at Daddy's. So is his bike. Please bring Daddy a new tie. He had to move away and get a new job. We miss Daddy.*
>
> *Next year, we will be at Daddy's big new house in Texas. We will have cookies for you and sugar for your reindeer when we are at Daddy's. We told our mother we don't want a tree, so please put my brother's presents on the kitchen table. I love you, Santa. I miss Daddy.*

"That same little person wrote this the following year."

> *Dear Santa:*
> *Please take my brother in your sleigh to Daddy's for Christmas.*
> *Mommy won't let him go. I will stay with her so she won't be mad*
> *at us. Daddy said he would bring him back. I told her I was asking*
> *you again to make us a family. She said you couldn't do that. I told*
> *her I didn't feel like making cookies with her. My brother needs new*
> *boots. I will leave his coat on the kitchen table.*

"What a caring little girl. Did you take her brother to Texas?"

"Her brother had the chicken pox. That was why he couldn't go to his father's. When I arrived, her mother had put up a small tree. I left the boots underneath it, along with some surprises for both of them."

"Did they have stockings?"

"Her mother hung them after the children went to bed. She wrote me a letter. I found it crumpled on the kitchen table.

> *Dear Santa,*
> *I'm sitting alone on Christmas Eve, and my thoughts are turn-*
> *ing back to when I was a child and anxiously awaiting your visit.*
> *I know my children are too young to comprehend all that has hap-*
> *pened. I fear they hate me, Santa. They don't realize that the divorce*
> *was out of my love for them. I had no choice. I couldn't stand his*
> *drinking anymore. I asked Meg to bake cookies with me. I told her*
> *we could leave some out for you. She ran to her room and slammed*
> *the door. I feel I did the best thing for them. I pray that someday they*
> *will understand. How I wish I still believed. How I wish there really*
> *was a Santa Claus."*

"Reading between the lines, Santa, I see the same situation being perceived differently. The daughter is hurt and angry. The mother is afraid and overwhelmed."

"Children see through youthful eyes. Most often, adults see through tired eyes."

"Your job is so important, Santa. You deliver more than toys."

"That's why the one chosen to assist the reindeer keeper is such a significant part of the plan."

"I know why you read me those particular letters, Santa. Our Meg wrote them. Now I understand what happened and why."

"She never asked for herself. She was hurt and protective of her father and brother. Her family had been torn apart, and she placed the blame on her mother. That's how she saw the situation as a child."

"I'm thankful she will be coming home." Abbey stood. "I must get back. Thank you for choosing me, Santa."

"You made the choices, Abbey. Choices—good and bad—do not go unnoticed."

"Please remember me as that little girl looking out my bedroom window."

Santa embraced Abbey, and whispered, "I see your mother carrying you to your bed, tucking you in, and kissing you gently."

"She loved me, didn't she Santa?"

"With her heart and soul your mother loved you, Abbey."

As Abbey turned to leave, Santa asked, "I don't suppose those are chocolate chip cookies in that bag?"

"Mrs. Claus said they were your favorite," laughed Abbey, handing Santa the biggest one. "They're my favorite too Santa."

Thomas was waiting. He held Abbey's hands. They were inside the barn in seconds. On her way back to the farmhouse, she decided to tell Steve about Santa Claus. They didn't keep secrets from each other, not even something as outlandish as a reindeer keeper. Abbey had no doubt he would believe her. She'd married a dreamer.

Chapter Fifteen

ABBEY DIDN'T FIND THE RIGHT TIME to tell Steve until nearly two weeks later. It happened on a Friday afternoon as they were on their way home from an appointment. The boys had insisted Abbey speak with doctors at a renowned cancer center close to the state line. She'd only gone for their sake. She'd already made up her mind she was staying with her doctor at the center not far from the house. Steve respected Abbey's decision. Anyone they asked had nothing but high praise for the local facility.

Realizing they'd be getting back later than planned, Steve pulled into a diner that looked like it was out of *Happy Days*.

"Hungry?" asked Steve.

"I could use a cup of coffee."

"Then this is the place."

"Have you been here before?"

"No, but these places always have great coffee and pie."

A sign greeted them, telling them to seat themselves. Steve led Abbey over to an out-of-the-way table with a view of a river rambling by. It wasn't busy. It wasn't the dinner hour yet.

"This reminds me of that diner we found in Maine on our honeymoon," said Abbey.

"I remember. We were surprised because they had live lobster on the menu. We—"

An older waitress with gray hair pulled up in a bun interrupted them, filling their glasses with ice water.

Steve took a sip. "We ate so much. Remember, Abbey? We went back to our room and fell sound sleep-on our honeymoon!"

The waitress came back with the menus. "I'll give you a few minutes."

"No need to," spoke Steve as he ordered the hot roast beef sandwich special. Abbey ordered a tuna fish sandwich on rye with a pickle and a bowl of tomato soup.

"It comes with a side salad, miss."

"Fine. And I'd like an endless cup of coffee."

"Make that two."

"You always order a tuna sandwich when you're nervous," Steve commented.

"Maybe the mercury in the tuna is calming!"

As they made small talk, a young couple with a little girl about three years old took a booth nearby.

"Look at the curls on that beauty, Abbey. I bet our daughter would have had curls like that."

"I wonder if she would have played the piano or taken ballet."

"Can you imagine her going out on dates? Her brothers would have been so protective."

"Not any more than you would have been, Dad."

"Having a daughter would have been a blessing, Abbey."

"She's our angel. Now we have Meg coming to live with us. I know it's hard to see, but a very caring person is under that hard surface."

"You had the tuna on rye with a pickle, soup, and a salad." The waitress again interrupted. "I'll keep the coffee coming."

It wasn't until the lemon meringue pie had been served that Abbey brought the conversation back to where she wanted. "I have something to tell you Steve. It has nothing to do with the cancer. In fact, I'm tired of talking cancer."

Abbey finally spoke of the reindeer keeper and meeting Santa Claus in the barn on Christmas Eve. She told him everything, including Santa reading the letters and giving her back the wooden box with painted flowers. She described the North Pole in detail, meeting Dancer and Mrs. Claus, and being inside the toy factory. She explained about the farmhouse. Ending with her duty of finding a replacement, Abbey put down her coffee and waited.

"She's leaving, Abbey. Look. She's waving bye to you."

Abbey turned and found the little girl with curly hair by her side.

"I'm sorry," spoke the mother. "She normally shies away from strangers."

"My thirty-plus years of teaching are showing." Abbey waved goodbye as the young family walked to the counter.

"It's not the teaching she's connecting to," spoke Steve. "It's you. Your spirit." Steve hesitated. "Don't speak in terms of finding a replacement to help Thomas. You're going to beat this. I need you. Santa Claus needs you."

"You needn't humor me by saying Santa Claus. Don't believe out of pity. I will not stand for any pity."

"I'd never pity you. I believe some things are unexplainable. The world needs a Santa Claus. What was it like to see him and talk to him?"

"I felt that freedom a child feels. I felt possibility again."

They lingered, sipping coffee and discussing the reindeer keeper.

"Think Santa would have any of my letters?" asked Steve.

"I'm sure he has them all."

"I don't remember writing to him."

"I'm sure you wrote letters."

"Only letters I remember writing were the ones from the war."

"Think back to when you were a little boy waiting on Christmas Eve. It's not an easy thing to do as an adult."

"I can tell you believe with your whole heart. Too bad we can't keep some of that feeling as we grow up."

"We do. It translates into faith. You have to have faith to get through what's thrown at you."

Steve agreed. He didn't tell Abbey his competition would be breaking ground soon with plans on being open before Christmas. She had enough on her mind.

"So considering what lies ahead, I mention a replacement to help Thomas only because I am the one responsible. It's like our having a will. It's putting things in order. It doesn't mean I'm giving up."

"When you put it in those terms, I understand." Tears swelled in his eyes. "I don't see my life without you."

"My heart still quickens when you walk through the door. What lies ahead is out of our control, Steve. That's where faith takes hold."

"Remember when we went skinny-dipping in that pond behind my parents' house?"

"We weren't even married. What were we thinking? It was in the afternoon!"

"I know what I was thinking,"

"The same thing I was thinking."

"I remain by your side every step of this journey, Abbey."

"That's why I confided in you about Santa Claus. But it has to stay between us. If any of it got out, I'd be locked away for good. The world is too full of cynics."

"The world needs a dose of compassion."

"Compassion is my criteria for a replacement."

"Is it Meg?"

"We had a glimpse of the real Meg at Christmas. Then after Santa read me some of her letters, I was convinced she's not what she pretends to be. I'll have to wait and see."

"That must be the Meg Eric fell in love with."

"Eric has a sense about him. I am so happy they're coming home."

"Speaking of home, look around, Abbey. The dinner crowd has come and gone, and here we sit."

"I wonder how many cups of coffee we've had!"

"Judging from the plates in front of me, I had two slices of pie!"

"It's time we literally roll out of here." Abbey headed to the restroom.

Steve paid their tab and returned to the table to leave a tip. The waitress was already clearing away the dishes.

"If you don't mind me saying, sir, you two make a lovely couple. I've met a lot of people over the years. I can tell a lot about a couple just by how they sit, how they look at each other. You two have it!" The waitress put the tip in her pocket. Picking up the plastic tub full of dirty dishes, she disappeared into the kitchen.

Steve waited for Abbey by the window. Geese were flying. The river was flowing.

"That waitress is right," he thought. "We do have it. But who knows for how much longer. Whatever would I do without her?"

Chapter Sixteen

THE MIDDLE OF MAY BROUGHT EVEN more flowers coloring the landscape. They were discovering trees they didn't know they had. Steve had rototilled an area near the house, hoping a garden might help keep Abbey's mind off her treatment. But after the second week of going to the clinic, Abbey was exhausted. That was when Meg stepped in. She and Eric were back. Although still getting settled, they were able to lend a hand. The big-box store had officially broken ground. The stage was set for more than one battle.

Eric met with a counselor at the school almost immediately. Most of his credits were accepted. He'd begin classes in September and work out a schedule with Steve. If all went as planned, he'd graduate in two years. Eric dug right in at the lumberyard. Since getting away from the grind of Wall Street, he seemed to be flourishing. With that two-year window, there'd be ample time to meet the competition head-on. Eric's connections had laid out a detailed plan for them to follow. The first day on the job, Eric began implementing it.

Meg took over as daughters do when necessary. She discovered a totally different side of herself, trading expensive manicures for hands that worked the soil. She loved gardening and tended to vegetable plants with enthusiasm, running in to tell Abbey of anything new sprouting. She read about canning and how to freeze vegetables. The kitchen was slowly becoming familiar to her. She spoke of finding a law firm at some point. For the moment, she felt needed.

Steve had reinforced the screens on the back porch, giving Abbey an out-of-the-way place with a daybed where she could retreat while still seeing everything going on. On good days she'd paint, but those became less and less.

Meg was the point person, taking Abbey wherever she had to be. She'd bring a notebook to write down what was said. Meg wanted to be sure to quote the doctors verbatim in case there were questions. A few times when Abbey had lost too much weight, they considered putting her in the hospital. Instead, after hooking her up to an IV, Abbey bounced back enough to go home. Abbey had made it clear to Steve at the beginning that she didn't want to be in a hospital unless absolutely necessary. They both had signed health proxies years back.

Being a daughter of a funeral director, Abbey had everything in order for her service and burial. When they lost the baby, they'd bought a cemetery plot not far from her parents. It also overlooked the meadow. The foothills could be seen in the distance. A friend of theirs tried to talk them into buying space in a mausoleum, but Abbey felt she'd get too claustrophobic. She liked being outside. Having lived with a man whose business was tending to the dead, cemeteries had always been part of the plan.

Just before Memorial Day weekend, Abbey woke to find her hair in clumps all over her pillow. A few days later, she was nearly bald. Steve kept repeating how beautiful she looked. He kept saying it wasn't her hair that he'd fallen in love with. Meg bought her lots of scarves. Once Abbey got used to wearing them, Meg went back and bought her a variety of earrings.

"You're a hippie again," Steve told her one evening that first week in June as they sat on the porch watching Eric and Meg in the garden.

"Well, if I'm one, you have to be one, too."

"Do I hear a challenge?"

"You do. I seem to recall how tight you wore your bellbottoms."

"And I seem to recall how much you liked them."

"I did."

"Not as much as I enjoyed those miniskirts of yours."

Abbey never heard Steve's last comment. She'd fallen sound asleep in his arms. Steve carried her upstairs and tucked her into bed, where she stayed until mid-morning. After returning from her treatment, she curled up on the daybed for the rest of the day.

That evening, Steve told Meg about an idea he had. "Let's surprise her this Sunday. We'll dress up as hippies. We can play some old tunes. Grill hamburgers and make her favorite—chocolate milkshakes."

"That's a great idea," replied Meg.

After bringing Abbey back home the next day, Meg went searching for some retro sixties clothing. She ended up at a thrift shop. She left with a bag full of clothing. When Sunday came around, they decided to wait until Abbey had her mid-afternoon nap. Meg's flowered miniskirt and hoop earrings impressed Eric. She'd teased her hair and wore pale pink lipstick. Steve and Eric strutted about in bellbottoms but both were more interested in the menu. With the Bee Gees ready to go, they waited for Abbey to wake up. When she did, she was violently ill.

After two hours of her wrenching on the bathroom floor, Steve couldn't take it any longer. With Eric and Meg helping, he carried her to their vehicle. As Eric drove, Steve held her in his lap. She was sick all the way to the hospital, crying, apologizing, and begging Steve not to leave her there. Meg tried to soothe her, but she herself was crying so hard she couldn't breathe.

They kept Abbey for three days. After that, she had but four weeks left of treatments. Sammy called toward the end of the month to say he and Cate were coming home for the Fourth. Without telling Abbey, Steve cancelled their cruise.

"We can do it another time," he told himself.

But deep down, doubts shadowed his optimism.

Chapter Seventeen

ABBEY FINISHED WITH THE CLINIC JUST before Sammy's arrival. She was told her hair might grow back in about a month or so and it could be curly despite the fact it had always been straight. They gave her an appointment six weeks out with no guarantees. Another MRI and more blood work were scheduled beforehand. It surprised Abbey to find how close she'd become with others at the cancer center. As she and Meg pulled away, professionals, along with fellow patients, were waving goodbye.

Thomas was coming back around. He'd stayed away while Abbey did what she had to do.

In private, he told her, "Santa and Mrs. Claus are keeping you in their prayers. You're welcome to come and visit the reindeer anytime, Miss Abbey."

"Thank you, Thomas. I've thought of you often. I'll be down after Sam and Cate leave. I have a favor to ask of Santa."

It wasn't long before Sam and Cate were sitting on the porch with Abbey. She had a hard time letting go of her son after thinking she'd never live long enough to see him again. He'd grown a beard. Cate took some shots of the two of them, one with too much hair and the other with no hair at all. Meg brought out lemonade, pointing out she'd used fresh lemons. Steve and Eric were grilling. It was a true Fourth of July celebration. In the evening, fireworks could be seen out beyond the barn. Sam had brought home his latest documentary, scheduled to air early

January in theatres. He wanted to be sure Abbey saw it. They made plans to show it the next afternoon which happened to be a Sunday. It'd be one of the last Sundays the lumberyard would be closed. Part of the new marketing plan included "Open Seven Days a Week."

Abbey excused herself early. She knew the next day would be busy. She wondered if she'd ever get her strength back.

When Abbey went down to the kitchen the next morning, she found Cate explaining to Meg about certain diets designed to combat certain cancers. "With your garden, you already have the perfect menu. Fresh fruits and vegetables with lots of whole grains are ideal. Stay away from refined sugars and processed foods, which you already do for the most part. You have one element of the holistic lifestyle."

"I've dabbled into holistic, but never took it too far," replied Meg. "I've found some good Web sites with great recipes for the vegetables we're growing. Every site raves about tomatoes."

"Tomatoes and blueberries. And don't forget onions," said Cate.

"You mentioned the vegetables would be one part. What are the others?" Abbey wanted to feel good again.

"Holistic includes the whole person: the spirit, mind, and body," said Cate.

"Once you feel stronger, we can start walking," said Meg.

"I'd like that. But don't let me hold you back from running."

"Running or walking, it doesn't matter to me," said Meg.

"I know we're only here through tomorrow, but I'll get online and find out more about diet. You might even consider yoga," said Cate.

"I've read in the paper about yoga classes being offered," commented Meg.

"I'll keep it in mind. But I have to take this a step at a time. And that means making myself go walking."

"We wish we could be here," said Cate. "Knowing you and Eric are here is so comforting, Meg."

"I can't imagine being anywhere else," replied Meg.

The day flew by. Sammy's documentary left everyone speechless. Cate told the family rumor was that the documentary could possibly be nominated for an Academy Award early next year. As everyone congratulated Sam, Abbey was trying to figure out in her head how many months away those awards would be. She didn't like thinking of her life in terms of minutes and hours, but that was reality.

As quickly as they came, it was time for Sam and Cate to leave. Abbey held back the tears clamoring to explode as she waved good-bye. She didn't want Sam to feel guilty. She knew if she gave her youngest any inkling that he may not see his mother standing on the porch steps in the morning light again, he'd never leave. But he had responsibilities. Abbey knew he had responsibilities. If anyone was aware what a crapshoot life is, it was Abbey. But now it was her life, not some stranger in a casket as she passed by on her way out the door.

Chapter Eighteen

MEG WAS A BLESSING. SHE PICKED up the slack without question. A few law firms called after hearing she was in the area, but she put them off. She told them she'd get back to them when she felt Abbey was out of the woods.

"If they're still interested, that's fine. If not, that's fine, too."

Eric thanked her on a daily basis for helping Abbey.

"She's like the mother I lost, Eric. It's a second chance."

Abbey and Steve felt blessed having Meg in the house. It gave them a sense of what it would have been like if their daughter had lived. Abbey was slowly feeling a bit stronger. She never made it back to the barn until one morning in late July. She'd just gone for a walk with Meg.

"You don't mind if I leave for a while, do you Abbey?" Meg was hoping to surprise Steve and Eric with lunch at the lumberyard. They'd been working hard getting plans in place. Ads were running. The service department was up to speed.

"I'm fine. Take a break. You've earned it."

Abbey showered and blended some vegetables for a drink. After covering her head, she walked down to the barn. She found Thomas with the horses.

Elated to see her, he did most of the talking. Of course, the reindeer were the center of their conversation. As they sat on bales of hay catching up where they'd left off, Abbey found it hard to think back before the

116

cancer. She hadn't realized how it'd swallowed her up and spit her out, like a tornado spinning out of control.

"I have a favor to ask, Thomas. I have a letter I'd like you to give to Santa. Tell him that as soon as I feel stronger, I'll visit him again."

"Your letter will be in his hands shortly, Miss Abbey."

Back home, Abbey thought she might try painting but decided maybe tomorrow. She fell asleep out on the porch as the hint of August approaching could be felt in the afternoon breeze. A knock on the screened door awoke her a few hours later. It was Thomas.

"Santa said to take your time with these. When you're finished, I'll return them to the Pole. He told me to tell you he's glad you're feeling better."

"Thank you, Thomas."

Abbey went to the kitchen. She poured a glass of iced tea, sat down at the table, and started reading what Thomas had handed her. It wasn't easy concentrating. She kept remembering Thomas' parting words.

"If they only knew how I really felt," she thought.

Noting Meg driving in, Abbey made a quick trip up the back stairs. She'd finish reading tonight and see Thomas sometime tomorrow, the day those awful tests began all over.

THEY WERE UP EARLY. ABBEY HAD to be at the hospital by eight. She'd been told to plan on spending the morning there. When Meg went to the restroom, Abbey made it clear to the head nurse that she alone was to be given the results. In confidence, she told the nurse of a radiating pain from her abdomen around to her back. Abbey had done some researching on the Internet. Although she had her suspicions, she needed them confirmed before saying anything to her family. Abbey left her cell number. When Meg returned, she was ready to go.

With the follow-up appointment still a few weeks away, Abbey knew when her phone rang a few days later, it wasn't good news.

"I understand. No. Keep that appointment, but I'd like to come in as soon as possible to talk to the doctor. That's fine. I'll be there at two tomorrow."

That night at dinner, she nonchalantly told everyone she was going to lunch the next day with some fellow retirees.

"There's no need to waste your afternoon toting me around, Meg. I think it's time I ventured out by myself."

"I think that's great. I told you everything would be okay."

Seeing that glint of hope in Steve's eyes nearly crushed Abbey. She excused herself and went to bed.

Chapter Nineteen

GUILT OVER HER DECISION TO SNEAK behind the backs of those she loved played havoc with Abbey until she turned into the medical building's parking lot. Sitting there, watching serious people in white coats hurry by, she knew it was because of those she'd left behind that she had to do this her way. Despite being the one stricken by the monster, she realized she'd be the one that would get her family through the darkness.

"Tell me the truth. Don't hold back. I want the truth."

It was just Abbey and her doctor sitting in his office overlooking a valley marked by fence posts as far as the eye could see.

"We can start treatments immediately, Abbey. You might consider palliative therapy. We'll do a biopsy. Once we get those—"

"How long do I have?"

"You're not listening to me, Abbey."

"You're not listening to me. This is my life. My *life*! I will say what is to be done to my body from here on out. I've been through a lumpectomy and radiation and endured your chemotherapy. I lost my hair. I've thrown up so many times I lost count. I threw up so violently that I fell on the bathroom floor. By God, I will be in charge until the bitter end. Now put a name to it, and give me my odds."

"The cancer is back, Abbey."

"It never went away. My body tells me the damn cancer never went away. I've been surrounded by death all my life. I was told for as far back as I can remember that death is part of life but this is *my* life; my only chance to breathe and laugh and sing and run and cry and contribute and love…."

"You have stage four pancreatic cancer," interrupted the doctor. "It has spread to the lymph nodes; your liver and lungs. Nothing's certain, but from my experience, you have, at most, six months."

It was one thing thinking it, but it was another thing hearing your life actually has an expiration date. Abbey looked around the room and tried to take in details that would have gone unnoticed a few seconds earlier, a small cloud chasing a larger one and the way the shade moved to the left and then straight out when the breeze came through the open window.

"Did you hear me, Abbey? I didn't mean to be so blunt. I thought that's what you wanted."

"I heard you. I needed to hear you say pancreatic cancer. I've said it over and over again in my head but hearing you say it out loud makes it real."

"We can take various avenues. Every case is individual."

"I've done the research. I ask that you minimize the pain as best you can. It will be hard enough on my family. I'll tell them before that scheduled appointment."

"I'm here to help in any way."

"You already have. I thank you for your honesty-and understanding. If Steve should call, be as honest with him as well."

Abbey glanced over at the receptionist on her way out. She noted the young woman's hair was up in a ponytail, just the way she'd worn her hair so many years ago. Abbey hadn't noticed that when she first came in. The world was now a stage for Abbey. She was out to take it all in for as long as she could.

Two days had passed since that meeting with her doctor. Abbey tried to start the conversation but the three of them were so upbeat about how well they thought she was doing that Abbey was beginning to think she'd just keep going until she no longer could go another inch.

She'd confided in Thomas. He had to go back inside the barn. Abbey found him brushing the runt. She stayed with him for the rest of the afternoon. He and Abbey had grown quite close.

During the evening of the third day, while sitting on the back porch listening to Steve suggest in a roundabout way that they should go on that European trip after all, Abbey realized there was no right moment. She had to speak up and make the moment. She owed them all the truth. The longer she put it off, the more plans they would make.

"I'll be right back." Abbey went into the kitchen. "Could you two join us?"

"More coffee, Abbey?" asked Meg.

"No thanks."

"Iced tea?"

"Sure. And please bring Steve a glass, too."

Abbey didn't give a damn about the tea. It was just easier. She had to get away from Eric. She had to get out of the kitchen. She feared that if she looked her son in the eye she'd fall apart. He was on cloud nine, just a few weeks away from going back to school. She made note to insist he continue with his plans regardless of her situation.

"My God," she thought, fighting back an onslaught of tears. "I'll never see him graduate."

After about fifteen minutes or so of listening to talk of more floor plans at the lumberyard, Abbey calmly put her tea down on the table and interrupted Steve as he was explaining how the aisles would be more customer-friendly.

"Did you need something honey?"

"How about a body rid of cancer?" she thought. "This is my moment. How should I start? How can I tell them?"

"I'll get whatever you need, Mom," said Eric. "You look so comfortable sitting next to Dad."

That simple statement almost changed Abbey's mind, but looking at the three smiling at her as if she was on the mend, reinforced her need to speak. So that is what she did.

"There are no words to say what I have to say. I've mulled it over in my head and played it back to myself in search of the right words. But there are none."

As the train's whistle drifted through the farmhouse, frightening terms caused sobs of disbelief. Questions of how and why had no answers. Meg collapsed in Eric's arms. It was a good half hour before Steve could speak. When he did, his voice cracked in pain. Emotions raced from anger to sorrow. Pleas to try new therapies and search for experimental groups came at Abbey faster than the train passing by beyond the mountains.

No one slept that night. It took a few more days before anyone could eat. Then Sam was called. He and Cate caught the next flight despite Abbey's telling them it was not yet necessary.

With everyone home, Abbey had company when it was time for her appointment. But they didn't hear what they wanted to hear. The doctor repeated what he'd told Abbey about each case being individual and there were procedures that could be tried. Cate asked about diet and holistic living. Meg threw in yoga and exercising. Eric suggested a second opinion. Steve remained silent as did Sam while the doctor went over stage four pancreatic cancer inside and out.

As they were leaving, he put it on the line. "We'll do whatever we can to keep you as comfortable as possible Abbey. I'm a phone call away any time of the day or night. I will see you weekly or daily. Whatever you need, Abbey, I'll be here for you. If you'd like a second opinion I will get on the phone today."

"No second opinion. I want to go home." Abbey's voice was strong. Although she spoke but a few words, it was understood what she was saying.

The doctor turned to those looking at him with desperate stares. "The odds are stacked against her but it doesn't mean you stop living your lives. You know Abbey. She wouldn't stand for that. There'll come a time when she'll need you more and more, but for now, she needs her space. She understands more than most that dying should be a dignified process. Abbey is calling the shots. When you think about it, that's all any of us could ask for. Go home. Cherish each moment."

That night, Eric cooked a pot of spaghetti and meatballs. His tossed salad with feta cheese and cut-up oranges was a hit, as was the toasted garlic bread. Surprisingly, everyone was starving, including Abbey. They cheered her few sprouts of returning hair. They cheered Eric for a great meal and wished him luck. Classes were getting closer. Steve told all kinds of stories, mostly about him and Abbey. Plans were made for another Christmas in the farmhouse. Sam told them they'd be home for Thanksgiving, too.

"I don't want you spending money you don't have on plane tickets or taking time from your work," Abbey told him.

"Just so happens we've decided to suspend filming November through mid-January. It's an expense thing at the other end."

It seemed to satisfy Abbey. She'd never know he'd be taking personal time while the filming continued. The next afternoon, Eric and Meg drove Cate and Sam to the airport. They had a hard time leaving. It was even harder for Abbey to say good-bye.

Chapter Twenty

AUTUMN USED TO BE ABBEY'S FAVORITE season, but not this year. The leaves were changing too fast, and the apples were falling too quickly. September was but a blur. October was halfway over. Knowing how much Steve had to deal with since Eric went part-time, Abbey acted better than she was feeling. At times, the pain was crippling. This charade came to an end on a blustery Tuesday afternoon when Steve arrived home earlier than expected. He found her curled up on top of their bed crying.

Realizing it was because of him that she hadn't said anything, Steve stayed in touch with the doctor on a daily basis from then on. He monitored her medications and went to every appointment and every test. He took the lead. He was resolute in keeping Abbey comfortable and providing her the best possible care. He, more than anyone, realized how important it was for her to be home. When Meg wasn't helping out at the farmhouse, she was at the lumberyard. Eric prepped her with what had to be done. The competition would definitely be opening their doors before the end of the year. While Steve's concern was evident, it took backseat to his Abbey.

Sam called daily. Thomas stopped in regularly with baked goods, explaining they were from a close friend. He always gave Steve a reindeer update for Abbey.

After handing Steve a tray of cookies one afternoon, he asked, "Could I see Miss Abbey for just a minute?"

126

"She's sleeping, Thomas." Seeing the disappointment on his face, Steve added, "Follow me. She might be awake by now."

Steve tried being quiet as he led Thomas up the back stairs, but it didn't matter for when he opened their bedroom door he found Abbey looking out the window. The sight of her lying there so pale and thin caught him off guard. It was all he could do to hold back the tears. But when she turned and looked at him with such love in her eyes, he knew what he had to do.

Walking over to her and bending down he whispered, "I have a surprise for you Abbey.

"I'd love a surprise."

"Thomas is here to see you."

A smile came to Abbey's face. That was all Steve needed. He led Thomas to Abbey's side and left them alone. A little over half an hour later, Thomas walked out of the room. "Thank you for the chance to see Miss Abbey. She is a wise woman."

He made his way back down the stairs and out the door. Steve never asked what they discussed.

With Halloween over, the cold was settling in, as was Abbey's incessant pain. She was in bed more than not.

One night at supper, Meg asked, "Could we turn the side porch into some sort of a bedroom for Abbey? Maybe enclose it with thermal windows? Then she'd be able to see the pasture and barn. We could take turns staying with her at night." That weekend, the porch was transformed into a bedroom resembling a page out of *Country Living*. Meg added the finishing touches. Two beds were in place. One was a hospital bed which the doctor recommended. Meg did her best to disguise it. When Monday evening came, Steve carried Abbey down the back stairs.

"Remember our honeymoon, Steve? That little cabin we rented and you carrying me through the narrow door. We laughed so hard that you almost dropped me."

"Remember the moose looking in the window? And the storm that came up from nowhere when we were in the canoe?"

Abbey hugged Steve a little tighter. "Don't let go of me. I'm not ready to say good-bye."

"Two things we promised, Abbey. We'd never keep secrets. We'd never say good-bye."

Later on, as he sat in the shadows while Abbey slept, Steve found himself wondering where the years had gone. To think of a time when she would be but a memory was too agonizing a place to go. Headlights dancing around the walls distracted him. He got up and saw that it was Thomas. Curious because of the hour, he grabbed his fleece and went outside into the first decent snowfall of the season. He hadn't planned on walking all the way to the barn, but he did. The smell of woodstoves in the distance reminded Steve of that cabin he and Abbey had referenced earlier. It had a woodstove, but heat was never anything they were lacking.

Thomas had left the barn door wide open. Steve assumed he was just running inside to check something so he waited by the truck. He was right. Thomas was back in minutes. Oddly, Steve's presence didn't surprise him.

"I have a sick one, Mr. Steve."

"So do I Thomas."

"I saw the new windows on the porch. Miss Abbey will like it there. She's a wee closer; able to see the land she's grown to love. We knew she would."

"Despite not knowing you for long, Abbey feels close to you, Thomas."

"We sometimes get to know someone in other ways, Mr. Steve. Good deeds transcend time."

"I never understood how we ended up living here. Abbey keeps telling me there's something very special about this place."

"Miss Abbey is a believer. Believers see possibility. That's why she was chosen. I must go. Have to get back for a quick visit with the boss about the sick one."

Instead of getting into his truck, Thomas went back inside the barn and shut the door.

On his way back to the farmhouse, Steve remembered a message Abbey had given him when he was carrying her down the stairs. It was for Thomas. She was asking about the runt.

"It'll just take a minute," thought Steve, turning back around. He'd find Thomas, relay the message and then get back to Abbey. "If she wakes up, I don't want her new surroundings to startle her," he reasoned.

Some of the lights were off in the barn, but it didn't matter. Although dulled by the falling snow, the moon guided Steve about the stalls. Because he didn't find Thomas right away, Steve figured he was with the reindeer.

"Thomas!" Steve called out.

But Thomas was nowhere to be found. Back outside, Steve walked farther down into the pasture and still no Thomas. Steve couldn't linger. While heading back to the house, the conversation he and Abbey shared in that diner came to mind.

"How could I have said anything else but that I believed, especially after Abbey described the North Pole and Santa Claus in detail?" he thought. "How could I have questioned when she spoke so passionately about those letters?"

While he went along with what she'd told him, of course, Steve knew the idea that Santa Claus could be real was impossible. He figured it was a distraction for her in dealing with what she had to confront.

But now, walking up the porch steps, something else Abbey had said stopped Steve in his tracks. "Thomas held my hands and took me to the North Pole."

"Where had Thomas just disappeared to?" Steve thought, looking back towards the pasture. "I searched the barn. I called out over and over again. Where is he? He said he was going on a quick visit to see the boss. He disappeared into thin air."

"He held my hands and took me to the North Pole," Abbey had said.

"Could there be truth in all that Abbey told me?" thought Steve.

Now Thomas' words were coming at him. "Miss Abbey is a believer. Believers see possibility. That's why she was chosen."

Standing on those steps, he looked inside at the woman who brought him joy and loved him beyond passion. Steve got it. He understood. Believers do see possibility. Abbey had been the one believing. If such a woman had faith in him as being a believer, then he too could erase that line of childhood passing into adulthood.

"Of course, there is a Santa Claus," Steve realized with such a force that colorful crystals mingling with snowflakes were falling all around him. "There has to be a Santa Claus. Why should growing up stop the wonder? It's even more important to believe as life swallows you up in worry. Abbey has faith in me. She knows me like no other, better than I know myself." Back inside, tears returned. "How I love her. It is her strength that will get me through," he thought.

Steve sat down next to Abbey. He brushed back wisps of hair, bent down, and kissed her forehead. He held her hand and whispered, "I believe, Abbey. I believe."

The wind seemed to carry his words. Abbey stirred. Opening her eyes, she reached up and pulled him near. "You've always been my believer."

From those words Abbey found strength. Unrelenting pain tried to subdue her spirit but couldn't. Not this time.

"I get it, Abbey. I understand what you told me. I believe in Santa Claus. I get it. I really do."

"I knew you would. Some things are meant to be, Steve. Remember?"

"I remember. I'll always remember my love."

Just then the wind let out a blast, whipping the snow against the windowpanes.

"It's snowing?"

"Coming down in buckets, honey."

Abbey motioned for Steve to move closer. She whispered in his ear.

"You what? You can't!"

"I can. I will. Help me up."

"But, Abbey."

"Help me. Get my coat, the wool one with the hood. My boots are in the back closet."

This sudden burst took Steve back to a few days before Eric was born. In the middle of the night, Abbey exploded with energy. She cleaned until dawn. There was no stopping her then and most certainly not now. If she wanted to bundle up, go outside, and make snow angels, he'd be right beside her.

The storm was letting up some as they headed into the night. Stars were beginning to peek through, showing them the way. Abbey chose the field closest to the barn. It was immense. The snow was untouched.

"Turn around. We need to be further apart. That's good, honey. On three, drop back into the snow. Try not to catch yourself with your hands."

"You sound like a snow angel pro."

"I am. After a snowfall like this one, Dad would take Jack and me outside. It was such fun when we were at his father's. The fields were massive. When we'd look out the next morning, snow angels were everywhere."

Planting her feet firmly in the snow, Abbey told Steve to do the same. She counted down, and back they went. Although he tried not to, Steve braced himself for the fall. His hand prints in the snow made for a strange looking angel. Abbey stayed in her bed while Steve tried again. Success! Now there were two angels.

"I'm amazed you never made snow angels."

"If I did, I don't remember."

"Start moving you arms up and down like this. When you're finished and want to make another, dig you feet in, sit up, and then jump to your feet."

"I'd rather stay put, Abbey. Two angels are sufficient. It's been the two of us for as long as I can remember."

"The years do seem to mesh, don't they? It's as if we were always one."

"We were, and we always will be. Do snow angels hold hands?"

"If we try hard enough, we can."

"That's what we've always done. We've kept trying even when things got tough."

"Like now?"

"Like now."

Steve stretched as far as he could and took hold of his angel's hand. They stayed there for a good hour, laughing and talking. Abbey showed Steve how to catch snowflakes with his tongue. They tried to count them as they floated down, but they couldn't keep up.

"I love winter, Steve."

"I know you do."

"Snow amazes me."

"I know it does."

"Please don't grieve, Steve. I'll be all around you."

Abbey fell asleep a few hours later. With so much fresh air, there was no need for another pill. Wrapped up in a blanket and sitting by the window, Steve decided there were three angels near: the two in the field holding hands and the one sleeping who believed in possibilities.

Chapter Twenty-One

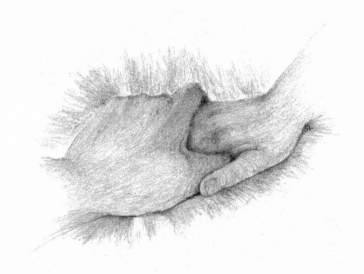

Sammy and Cate arrived a few weeks later after hearing how strong a dose of morphine the doctor had prescribed; how much weight Abbey had lost, and how much pain she was still enduring. Steve brought in hospice. It was more for the family than Abbey. If anyone understood death, it was Abbey.

Steve stayed every night with her despite the boys telling him he needed his rest. Abbey's only request was that he read to her so that is what he did even when she was sleeping. His choices came from children's books she had collected over the years. She had shelves full of them.

A week before Thanksgiving, the big-box store opened. It came as a relief, having loomed over their heads for what seemed an eternity. Because of the marketing in place, the lumberyard held its own. Eric thought about taking a leave from his classes, but Meg insisted he stay in school. She and Cate helped at home while Sam did what he could at the lumberyard. They all pitched in, allowing Steve the time necessary to be with Abbey. He was determined to keep Abbey home. He'd made a promise.

Despite the circumstances, Eric prepared a scaled-down Thanksgiving meal when that day arrived. No one felt like eating. Thomas stopped with more gifts of food and asked that Steve relay his love and that of his family's to Abbey. He also wanted Abbey to know the runt had grown into a fine reindeer.

134

"Soft as ever, tell her. Tell Abbey her little runt might be chosen this year."

Abbey was restless. The pain was intensifying. Her medication had been increased. A quiet evening snowfall seemed appropriate as they gathered together on that side porch. Steve had asked their priest to stop and join them in prayer. A few hours later, Steve told the nurse readying Abbey for the night that she could leave after Abbey settled down. He'd call her if need be. With the farmhouse quiet, everyone asleep, and the snow sprinkling about, Steve sat by Abbey's side and talked to her despite the fact her medication kept her asleep. He recalled the first time he set eyes on her and laughed at how awkward he felt asking her to dance. He thanked her as he often did for getting him through Vietnam. He admitted he feared he might never see her again. He praised her for their beautiful children. He conveyed Thomas' message about the little runt. Over and over, he told her not to worry about him. He told her he would carry on, knowing she was out of pain and at peace with their daughter. There were no words he could find to tell this woman how much he loved her. He didn't have to. Somehow, out of the depths of sleep and pain, Abbey lifted her hand. With Steve taking hold, she pulled him close. As he wept and as those snowflakes she loved swirled and colored crystals lit the dark, Abbey died in the still of the night.

Not far away, reindeer lowered their heads. A good friend turned and walked back inside the barn as stars seemed to sparkle all the more, shining down on two angels holding hands.

Chapter Twenty-Two

IF EVER A FUNERAL WENT LIKE clockwork, it was Abbey's. She'd spent an afternoon with the man who'd bought the funeral home. She knew what she wanted, right down to which parlor she was to be laid out in for one evening only of calling hours. Steve worried they might not be able to go to the cemetery. He feared the cold weather may have deterred her burial, but he worried for nothing. There had been a break in the weather.

A little after two o'clock on a rather pleasant November afternoon, Abbey was laid to rest next to her baby, overlooking the meadow with the foothills in the distance and her parents nearby. Jack had called. In Asia on business, he was unable to make it home. He sent flowers and shared his intentions of getting back over the summer. That evening, after friends and family said their good-byes, Meg carefully cut out copies of Abbey's obituary from the paper. Following Abbey's instructions, Meg placed one in the funeral director's file. She put one in the nightstand on Steve's side of their bed and made sure Eric and Sam each had a copy to put away for safekeeping. Abbey had written her obit, sitting on the side porch one afternoon as leaves were falling.

Sam and Cate stayed another five days. Before leaving, they made plane reservations to return for Christmas. Eric promised they'd have a real tree despite their father saying this might be the year to get an artificial one. The boys knew he wasn't up to a Christmas without Abbey. At the same time, they knew their mother would have insisted they have a tree from their woods, just as they did the year before.

Sam was relieved Eric and Meg were home. It made his leaving a little easier. It was a little less to worry about when he was way across the country. Abbey had been encouraging Meg to turn the front parlor into an office. Steve thought it was a great idea. She could open her own law firm and, at the same time, be available to the reindeer keeper once she took over Abbey's duties. When that would be was not up to Steve.

Meg took charge of the coming holiday. Abbey had prepped her, told her where everything was and where everything went. On the last Sunday before Christmas, Thomas stopped by to say he'd found them a Christmas tree. With Eric's encouragement, they followed Thomas into the woods. Steve didn't say much until he saw the tree.

"You sure know Miss Abbey, Thomas. This tree is perfect."

"Miss Abbey told me about the Christmas tree you had the first year you were married. She said it was so big that it wouldn't fit into your small apartment."

"That apartment wasn't small. It was tiny."

"Where was it, Dad?"

"Near Charleston. Your mother met me there when I got back from Nam. We eloped immediately. We couldn't stand to be apart another day. That apartment was all we could afford, but it didn't matter. We had each other."

"Miss Abbey told me she worked in a movie theatre. She'd get a discount so you two would go to the movies at least once a week."

"Then we'd go next door for a hamburger and Coke."

"Sounds good to me, Dad," said Eric.

"We were lucky. We didn't have a penny, but yet, we had what no amount of money can buy."

The wind was picking up. It was sifting through branches like sand on a beach.

Steve walked over to get a closer look. "Look at the pinecones! Abbey would have gone on and on about the tree having......" Steve broke down. He couldn't complete the sentence.

No one knew what to say. It was Thomas who spoke.

"I feel her beside us, Mr. Steve."

"Angels are always near Thomas."

Turning back towards the tree, Steve continued, "Could you help me bring the tree out of the woods?"

"I'll be at the barn by seven tomorrow morning, Mr. Steve."

"I'll be there at six forty-five!"

On their way back to the house, Steve started talking about Christmas. Meg told him how she and Abbey had discussed the menu to go with the prime rib and the stockings she'd packed away. Eric again told Steve when he had to pick Sam and Cate up at the airport. Ideas were exchanged. Midnight Mass was a given.

"Maybe before Christmas dinner we could go to the cemetery, Eric," suggested Steve.

"I know Mom-and Grandma and Grandpa too-would like that, Dad."

"Your mother was the spitting image of her mother. They were beautiful women. It must run in the family."

Meg pulled on Eric's coat sleeve, speaking to him with her eyes.

"Okay, Meg. I know. Okay. You're right, honey." Eric paused. "Dad!"

Steve and Thomas had gone ahead.

Eric called again. "Dad, wait up!"

"Did I forget something? Your mother always took care of Christmas."

"No, you didn't forget a thing. Mom would be proud of you. It's … it's just … we have something to tell you."

"Right here?"

"I can't think of a better place." Meg smiled.

"I'm listening."

"With Mom dying and everything going on at the lumberyard, we've been waiting for the right moment to tell you. You're going to be a grandfather. We're expecting a baby, Dad. We are going to have a baby!"

The thought of new life overtook those still grieving. Tears were back, but they were happy ones.

"I know you're thinking about Mom. I know you're thinking how much she would have loved being a grandmother," said Eric.

It was snowing a little harder as Steve embraced the parents-to-be. "I'm so happy for you. What a beautiful blessing. Your mother knows." Steve watched the snow coming down. "She is right here with us."

Talk of names and getting the crib out of the attic, and teasing Eric about going into the delivery room led them back to the farmhouse. Meg made hot chocolate. Even Thomas stayed for a cup. Steve dug out the boxes full of tree decorations. Inside one were those stockings-all four of them.

"Mom would have had fun filling a stocking for the baby," said Eric.

"Maybe we should put one out and see what happens," said Steve.

"'Tis a magical time for sure, Mr. Steve." Thomas winked.

"Abbey was right again," thought Steve. "Christmas is for believers, no matter what their age."

That thought would soon prove true again.

Chapter Twenty-Three

HAVING PUT CHRISTMAS ON THE BACK burner up until learning he was going to be a grandfather, Steve quickly made up for lost time. With less than a week to go and feeling Abbey with him every step of the way, Steve prepared the family for the holiday. The tree was up and decorated. It sat in the same spot as the year before. Eric had the kitchen under control. Not many gifts were being bought. This year, more than any other Christmas, was about family gathering. Eric did order a cradle handmade by the Amish. To keep it a secret, he arranged for it to be delivered to Thomas. They'd keep it in the barn until Christmas Eve. Business at the lumberyard was steady despite an onslaught of glitzy sale flyers from the competition. The boys felt their mother had a lot to do with it. Her power of prayer seemed to be stronger than ever.

When Christmas Eve arrived, Eric and Meg were on the road by six. If Sam's flight was on time, they'd be back mid-afternoon. The weather was clear, and so were the roads. Closing the lumberyard early, Steve got home when the house was quiet. With Christmas on his shoulders, he wanted to do his best to make it memorable. He never realized how much Abbey had done in preparation. Because of Abbey, Steve bought the baby a Christmas stocking. Not only did he buy stocking stuffers for the little one, he bought them for everyone. He even took the time to wrap each small gift.

After checking what Eric had left slowly cooking Steve went back outside to do a little shoveling. He didn't get too far. He saw Eric's Tahoe driving in. They were home for Christmas.

Abbey would have been so proud of them. Tears were shed, both in celebration of her memory and the baby due in early July. Meg and Cate brought out the dishes. Steve lit the candles. Before enjoying Eric's feast, they all gathered about the magnificent tree with tiny pinecones. Cate took lots of pictures. She promised Abbey she would.

Just as they sat down to eat, Thomas' headlights could be seen going down to the barn. Steve looked over at Meg passing the potatoes and realized how busy she was going to be. There certainly were many miracles in the works.

When dinner was over, they gathered again around the tree, waiting for midnight Mass. Meg was exhausted, but insisted on going with everyone to the old French church. By the time they got back to the farmhouse, it was close to one thirty. They were in bed by two.

Restless, Meg came back down for a cup of tea, unaware Steve was in the front room filling the stockings. He stayed quiet, thinking this was the time. He could hear the water running and made out the clicking of the cup on the saucer. He waited a few more minutes and heard the refrigerator door open. Then he heard the saucer clank in the sink. But instead of anything happening, the kitchen light was turned off. Meg went back upstairs.

"Maybe her inheriting the duties of the reindeer keeper will happen when I go to bed," he thought. "Maybe everyone needs to be asleep."

As he was about to turn out the tree lights, a sudden brilliance drew Steve's attention to the far window overlooking the backfields. It was the moon, mingling with colorful sparkles swirling over the land. Awestruck, Steve stood and watched. He noticed the barn lit up as never before. Without hesitating, he was out the back door and on his way through the snow with no coat, boots, or hat. He wasn't cold in the freezing temperature. When he arrived at the barn, he wasn't surprised to find Thomas waiting for him.

"Come in, Mr. Steve. We've been waiting for you."

Steve stepped inside without hesitation. He followed Thomas past the sheep and horses.

Once in front of the door leading into the reindeer stall, Thomas stopped and turned back around. "Do you believe, Mr. Steve? Do you believe?"

Steve understood the question. He'd been aware of Thomas' disappearing into thin air that night he'd walked to the barn. He listened to Abbey tell of what she witnessed. He'd accepted the concept that there had to be a Santa Claus, if for no other reason than the world sorely needed to believe in the wonder of it all.

Standing there on Christmas Eve, Steve let go of worries and sorrows. Gone went his despair over Abbey's suffering and death. Gone went his worry over the competition. Gone went the sadness over losing a child. Steve found himself back at a place he'd long forgotten.

He was seven on a Christmas morning. With his daddy fighting in Korea for almost a year, Steve had taken on the impossible task of trying to fill the shoes of this man he considered to be a tower of strength. The middle child, Steve grew up between two sisters who quarreled more than not. He didn't understand why but he knew how much his mother worked. She was away most of the time. They had lots of babysitters. Occasionally Steve was left alone. When it was very late, Steve sometimes heard his mother coming home. And he sometimes heard her crying.

This particular holiday had gone fairly well despite the fact his older sister had to beg their mother to get out of bed Christmas morning. She had worked extra late. Santa hadn't filled their stockings. Their mother explained he had other children to visit who needed more than they did. Steve didn't mind. He thought it was a nice thing for Santa to do.

Steve recalled how excited he'd been waiting for the one thing he'd asked Santa Claus to bring him. He knew what he'd asked for couldn't be wrapped and put under the tree. Any minute he thought his father would walk through the door. He kept watching out the window. He listened for a car to pull up and a door to slam shut. That's all he'd asked for this Christmas. He'd written to Santa, telling him how much he missed his father, how his sisters fought, how his mother was never home, and how hard it was to go to school or play with friends without his father near.

Steve was ready. He'd cleaned his room and did all the shoveling. But it never happened. Despite the matchbox cars and a few other things he'd received, Steve went to bed that Christmas night wondering if there was a Santa Claus. Around three o'clock, he heard his bedroom door open and familiar footsteps walk toward him. He felt those strong arms scoop him up and the shadow of a beard rub against his cheek. His father still smelled of licorice cough drops. His voice was still deep and assuring, telling his son how much he'd missed him.

His father stayed with them for over two weeks. They went skating and sledding down the hill just outside of town. Steve's mother stayed home with them. His sisters stopped fighting. They were a family again.

Steve plugged into that moment. He believed. Who else but Santa could have brought his father home from a war halfway around the world just when he needed him?

"I believe, Thomas. I do believe."

A faint jingling of bells floated about the barn as Steve followed Thomas through the doorway. The sight was amazing. Cedar and pine boughs were wrapped about the wooden posts. Wreaths decorated the windows. Most amazing was the towering tree adorned in strings of wild berries and acorns. Those bells were getting closer. The reindeer were on alert. Barn cats hid.

Thomas signaled for Steve to move aside as he approached the back of the stall. Just as he'd done so many times before, Thomas took a final look around, slid the latch up, and pushed with all his might. This year, the door opened without a hitch. Inside came the wind. Inside came more crystals swirling around the old structure. It was how Abbey had described this very moment that day in the diner. The jingling stopped. And just as Abbey recounted the wonder of what happened next, Steve felt the same as he looked into the eyes of Santa Claus himself.

"Oh, Abbey!" he wanted to shout. "He is as you said he was. Taller and plumper; his beard does seem whiter and fuller. His cheeks are a deeper red, much like his velvet suit."

Steve stepped back a bit and watched as Santa approached his reindeer. Abbey told of how he petted each one while checking the might of their antlers and width of their legs. That's exactly what he was doing with Thomas right behind. While Santa went from one reindeer to the

147

next, elves came scurrying inside carrying packages and placing them under the tree. Steve knew they were Thomas' family. He also knew who'd baked the cookies being brought in and placed atop a long table Thomas had decorated.

After visiting the last of the reindeer, Santa began selecting which ones would go with him on the journey. Steve stood watching as those chosen were led outside. Santa's reindeer team was soon in place. Steve had been so enthralled that he didn't notice Santa standing by his side.

"Abbey told me you were a believer, Steve. Looking into your eyes, I see that too."

"But Santa, I thought it would be Meg. Abbey told me of her letters. She was confident in her abilities."

"Walk with me, Steve." They went into the night. Santa continued talking. "You are right. Meg was on Abbey's list. But so were you."

They stopped in front of the sleigh. Santa continued. "Sit with me before I go."

Abbey had told Steve how massive the sleigh was, bigger than any picture book illustration she'd ever seen. The leather reins lying on the seat fascinated Steve, as did the bag of toys filling the back end. The reindeer were in place. They were anxious to get going.

"Windier than usual. I'll have to climb a little higher to make some headway. No flight is ever the same. Tonight reminds me of my quick trip back to Korea."

"Korea?"

"To get your father. I had to go back. I couldn't get in on the first try. That's why he was late getting home to you."

"But how did you pull it off in the middle of a war? What did my father say? How did he get clearance? How did you land?"

"All those answers come with believing, Steve. Time can stand still if you believe. He was out of Korea and back without being missed."

"But why did you go there? Couldn't he have taken a leave?"

"You asked me to bring him home for Christmas. When a child writes me a letter, it is written in pure belief. You didn't ask the how. You didn't need the details. You had faith in me." Santa paused. "As you've been reminded by the loss of your Abbey, life doesn't always work out the way we see it, but then we don't always see the bigger plan. Believing gives us the faith needed when we are tested. Abbey chose you because you've earned this honor. Meg is young. Her turn will come. But you've proven your goodness over and over again." Santa reached under the seat and pulled out that rather large satchel. "Come with me." He jumped down off the sleigh. "I have something to share with you."

Back inside, Steve realized Thomas knew Santa would return. In place were two chairs next to the tree, along with a small table holding Santa's pipe and two cups of hot chocolate.

Santa remarked, "Thomas, it appears you've had a wonderful time with your family."

"Indeed, Santa," smiled Thomas. All the gifts were opened. Thomas and the other elves continued chatting and eating cookies as Steve sat down with Santa.

Tears were streaming down Steve's face even before Santa spoke. "But Santa, I'm not a true believer. I try. I told Abbey I was. I told Thomas the same, but I'm not a true believer because I haven't accepted Abbey's death. I miss her more than I can put into words. Some days I'd rather stay in bed than face another day without her, but I can't. I have Eric and Meg at home. Sam and Cate rely on me. And now Abbey and I are going to be grandparents. I don't deserve the honor Abbey has extended me."

Santa took a sip of his hot chocolate, lit his pipe, and thought for a moment before speaking. "Believing doesn't mean we can't feel life's emotions. Grieving is a process. If you weren't a believer, you couldn't feel the loss, shed the tears, or absorb the grief. The acceptance you speak of comes in time. The pain will soften. Memories will fill your heart. The sadness will turn to joy in the new life coming. This child will not be a substitute, but a testament to the love you and Abbey shared. You are a true believer, Steve."

Santa reached into his satchel and pulled out letters held together by a ribbon. Undoing the ribbon, he adjusted his glasses. "You wrote this when you were seven."

Dear Santa,
Mommy is sad. I am, too. Daddy is gone. He might get hurt. I

149

have to help Mommy. I will, Santa. I don't want Daddy to be hurt. My sisters are sad, too. They fight a lot. Mommy is at work a lot. It is hard to go to school or play with my friends. I miss my family. Please bring my Daddy home for Christmas. He is far away in a war. Daddy always takes me sledding down the big hill the day after Christmas. My sisters go too. I know Daddy will be sad if he can't take us. Thanks Santa. Be careful.

   Love,
   Steve

"I don't recall writing that, Santa."

"With your father being away, many responsibilities were forced on you. At such a young age you had to be the man of the house so I'm not surprised you don't remember writing me. Your childhood was cut short."

"I don't remember much about my father. When I do go back there in my mind, I feel a tremendous sadness. My life began when I met Abbey."

"I understand you were a good football player in high school."

"My grandmother always told me I had my father's style out on the field."

"Looking at you now, Steve, you remind me of him. When your father was a little boy he'd fall asleep near the Christmas tree waiting for me."

"That's what our Sammy used to do!"

"I remember. I almost woke Sam up more than once while filling his stocking."

Realizing the time, Santa unfolded another letter. "I have one more to read. You were eight when you wrote this."

Dear Santa,
   I wish it was last year. You brought my dad back home. We had a good time. I was sad when he left. He didn't come home again. He died in that war, Santa. Mom gave me his flag. She told me I really have to help her now. She cries all the time. She gets mean so I stay

in my room a lot. I think she is mean because she is tired. Please bring her something pretty. My sisters are mean, too. They are just sad. Please bring them something nice. I love you, Santa. Thanks for bringing Daddy home for Christmas last year. We had fun sledding.
Love,
Steve

Santa was the first to speak. "You grew up a believer, Steve. You've worked through loss all your life and you will do so again. Abbey told me she'd married a dreamer. She sent me a message when she was so sick, asking if she could read some of your letters. I shared what I've read to you with her. She believed in you, Steve. As she told me, you always see the goodness in people. She was right."

"I kept that folded flag beside my bed. Some nights, I would cling to it as my sisters fought or my mother came in from work, late and tired. Looking back now, I understand some of what my mother was feeling. Those were different times for a working woman. She had no family that would help her. She worked so hard providing for us and keeping us in that house that had always been our home. She died while I was in Vietnam. She couldn't deal with another war. It was too painful, too frightening. I only wish I could have been there for my parents when they passed. I am so thankful that Abbey and I had time to say good-bye."

"What you and Abbey had will live on, Steve. What your mother dealt with is heartbreaking in a tragic sense. Judging parents through youthful eyes is often distorted. Walking in someone's shoes is the equalizer."

Santa folded the letters and put them back inside the envelope. As if on cue, Thomas was at his side. Santa stood, adjusted his belt, and finished the last of his hot chocolate.

"Abbey made a fine choice, Steve."

Thank you for believing in me, Santa. Merry Christmas."

Steve followed Santa and Thomas back outside.

"I thank you, Steve. The world needs more dreamers." Santa climbed aboard his sleigh and made one last check. "We are ready to begin our Christmas Eve flight. Merry Merry Christmas to all."

With a snap of his wrists, the sleigh was up and amongst the glistening stars. In an instant, it disappeared behind the moon.

"I am happy it is you, Mr. Steve. Miss Abbey was not only kind but smart."

"Thank you, Thomas. Whatever you need, I will be here for you." Steve checked his watch and noticed it hadn't budged. He also realized he was without a coat or boots.

"You've been in the presence of Santa Claus, Mr. Steve, which means you are a believer in the wonder of it all."

"I understand, Thomas. I now understand."

"Did you notice, Mr. Steve?"

"Notice?"

"Miss Abbey's little runt is the new Dancer this year. She is right behind Rudolph. 'Tis for sure a most magical time."

"For sure, Thomas. A magical time for sure."

At every step taken back to the farmhouse, Steve saw Abbey, painting the flowers, walking the backfields, waiting for him on the porch.

"Merry Christmas, my love," he whispered as glistening snowflakes surrounded him. "You are in my heart forever."

Steve turned out the lights and went upstairs to bed. He fell sound asleep remembering that little boy waiting for his daddy so many Christmas Eves ago.

Chapter Twenty-Four

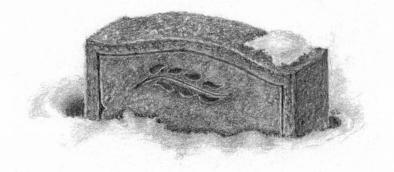

STEVE WAS UP AND OUT SHOVELING long before anyone else was awake. He remembered Abbey telling him how rested she was last Christmas morning despite all she had on her mind. Steve now understood what she meant. Eric soon joined him for coffee. They discussed fatherhood. Eric talked of his excitement and his worries. Steve shared his story about his own father coming back from Korea on Christmas. Eric seemed to appreciate hearing about a grandfather he never knew.

Breakfast was the traditional. When it was time for the gifts, they were all happily surprised to find the stockings filled. The littlest one received the greatest response.

"You were smart, Dad. You chose yellow instead of blue or pink," remarked Eric.

"When your mother and I were having children, finding out if it was a boy or a girl wasn't an option. It was always a surprise. I liked that. But I can see the advantages of knowing ahead of time. It just takes the surprise element out of the equation."

"We've decided we don't want to know. We like surprises, too," spoke Meg, still surprised by the beautiful cradle.

"You did a great job shopping, Dad," said Sam.

"Your mother trained me well."

Indeed she had. Steve was on his feet as soon as the last gift was opened. The room was picked up. Gifts were put under the tree. After

Eric had the dinner under control, they headed down the snowy road to the cemetery. This year, Steve led them around the tombstones.

"It seems like we were just here, Dad," said Eric. "I can't believe a whole year has gone by."

"In some ways, it seems like only yesterday; in others, an eternity Eric."

"This is the perfect place to tell all of you that I'm scheduled to begin work on a new documentary after the Academy Awards. It came about as a result of coming here last Christmas," announced Sam. "Listening to what Mom was saying about cemeteries and dying and how many untold stories are laid to rest without being heard, I pitched the idea to some investors, and they bought it. We've already started scouting cemeteries."

"In this country, Sammy?" asked Steve.

"Not only in this country, but in this very location, Dad."

"I remember hearing stories about some who are buried here that were generals and great musicians. There are even famed artists and scientists."

"Actually, Eric, I went back and forth with those investors about that very point. I'm not looking for the famous. I'd prefer featuring people, everyday people who made a difference in their own quiet way. Those are the people whose stories need to be heard for they are just as or even more inspiring."

"I agree, son," said Steve. "We can all think of people who've impacted our lives and the lives of so many others just by being themselves."

"That's why I'd like to include Mom. If it wasn't for her knowledge of and respect for the process of dying and her belief in death as part of life, I never would have thought to roam about cemeteries to find stories about life and living. I never understood her obsession with obituaries, but she was right. We'll all have one. We know the beginning. We have no control over the last date entered, yet we do have influence on the in-between. I think this documentary could be powerful. Make people think of their own mortality and responsibility to tap into their God-given abilities. That's our mission with the project."

The wind shifted. A muffled ringing drew their attention to the fields beyond the headstones.

"There's that sleigh from last year. Look! The same two horses are pulling it." Cate took some shots with her camera.

"I wonder if they remember this family that visits cemeteries on Christmas," Eric laughed.

"All families have their traditions. I'm into visiting cemeteries now. You never know what or whom you are going to discover," replied Sam.

They paid their respects to Abbey's parents. As they moved nearby to wish Abbey a Merry Christmas, Steve talked about the baby they'd lost.

"We were devastated. We would have had a daughter. Although we accepted God's will, we always wondered about her."

"We would have had a sister, Sammy," said Eric.

"Our baby would have had an aunt," said Meg.

"There are so many what-ifs. That's why your mother was such a wonderful partner. I never questioned her love. I think including your mother in your documentary is a well-earned tribute, Sammy. Growing up as a funeral director's daughter gave her a unique perspective on life."

They knelt by Abbey's grave overlooking the meadow with the foothills in the distance, and joined in prayer. Then they each took a moment to speak.

"We have so much to tell you, honey. Your eldest son would like to be first."

"I can't explain how I feel when I'm in my cooking classes. I took your mother's cook book with me one day, and we made a few of the recipes she had marked. Everyone loved them. Thanks, Mom, for encouraging me. You were right. The hardest part of any decision is making it. I love you, Mom."

It was Cate's turn. "You'd be so proud of everyone, Abbey. Your traditions guided us through today. The stockings were filled. The prime rib is cooking just the way you'd cook it, and the cheesecakes are in the freezer. Oh! I forgot. The tree! The tree has tiny pinecones all over it. I took pictures of everything. I'll make sure everyone gets copies. Thank you for Sammy. I'm so blessed, Abbey."

Holding Cate's hand, Sammy began. "I'm too am blessed Mom. You taught me about owning one's passion. For you it was obits. What intrigued you was that space between birth and death. You'd remind Eric and me that it was up to us to fill in our personal space. Passion is individual, Mom. Without even realizing it, I've pursued mine because of something you did every day. Ironically our passions will soon intertwine. Love and miss you, Mom. You are with me wherever passion takes me."

It took Meg a few minutes. "Every time I look out the window, I imagine how you'd paint the scene. The snow is knee deep in some places. Our conversations stay with me, Abbey, which brings me to our news. Eric and I are going to have a baby in July. Can you believe it? I will be a mother. I feel a love I never thought possible. I'm starting to appreciate my mother, Abbey. It's complicated, as you know. Thank you for your guidance. Thank you for believing in me."

The two couples quietly got to their feet and left Steve alone with his Abbey.

Taking off his glove, Steve wiped some snow off her tombstone and followed the groove etched in marble spelling out her name. He lifted his head, shut his eyes, and allowed the wind to free his mind as he went back to days gone by. Telling her in mere words what she meant to him was impossible, so he summed up those years, days, hours, and minutes by simply telling Abbey he loved her. He thanked her for sharing her mind, soul, and body. He thanked her for their three children. He thanked her for entrusting him with the duties in the barn. He thanked her for being his snow angel. He went on to say she'd been right in her description of Santa.

"The sleigh with the reins and toys waiting to be delivered amazed me, Abbey. The reindeer keeper asked that I tell you Santa chose the little runt to be Dancer—part of his reindeer team."

Steve needed to catch his breath. So many memories filled his heart.

"Can you believe it, honey? We're going to be grandparents." Turning his head away, Steve dug inside his coat pocket for his handkerchief. Wiping his eyes, he continued. "Santa read me the letters I wrote to him. He told me you read them too. I haven't thought of that Christmas after my father died in so long. I realize now it's too sad to go back there. He was a good man and a good father. He would have loved you, Abbey. Eric reminds me of him. Our son will be a wonderful father."

Steve could say no more. He ended where he began, "I love you, my Abbey. I always will."

Steve kissed her headstone, cleared away more snow, and headed back toward the waiting vehicle. Little snowbirds flickered through the cemetery as off in the distance the train sang its soulful song.

Chapter Twenty-Five

ERIC AGAIN PROVED HIS TALENT IN the kitchen. They all went back for seconds before retiring for the night. The house quieted down around nine-thirty. Steve settled into the front room and sipped a glass of wine with only the tree lights on. The wind hadn't let up. He was hoping it would, as Sam and Cate had to leave in the early morning. Looking at the decorations hanging in front of him, Steve remembered when most had been made. He could hear the boys laughing and Abbey praising them for their creativity. He remembered Abbey staying up late sewing decorations just for Eric and Sammy. There were cows and pigs, and teddy bears. Some were small; others were rather large. They all had the year scribbled on them somewhere.

He got up to refill his glass. As he did a knock at the back door took him by surprise. Steve peeked through the dining room window and noted it was Thomas. On came the kitchen light as he unlocked the door.

"Come in, Thomas. It must be below zero out there."

"Doesn't matter, Mr. Steve. It's Christmas."

"That it is. Would you like some cheesecake?"

"No thank you, Mr. Steve. Miss Abbey wanted me to give this to you tonight. She asked me to tell you to put it in the wooden box sitting back on the shelf behind the tree. Good night, Mr. Steve."

Steve put his glass on the counter and looked down at what Thomas had handed him. It was a ribbon. At first, he didn't recognize it, but then it clicked. This ribbon held together his letters to Santa. His heart began to quicken as he walked back into the family room. He turned on a light and approached the tree. Looking in toward the shelves, Steve saw the wooden box. He remembered Abbey telling him about the box, but he never took hold of it until now.

Steve sat on the sofa and placed the box in his lap. There were those beautiful flowers Abbey had painted when she was a little girl with her mother by her side. On its backside was Abbey's autograph. Steve slowly opened it. There curled about neatly was another ribbon. He pulled it out of the box and as he did his memory went back to last Christmas. He envisioned Thomas handing it to Abbey. Steve knew where it had come from. Deciding Abbey wanted him to put his ribbon with hers, he wound them up together and went to place them inside the box.

That's when he noticed something else. There were two letters. One envelope had his name on it. Abbey had left Steve a letter in the wooden box with the flowers painted on it. The other was that letter Abbey's mother had written to Santa Claus.

Seeing Abbey's penmanship and reading "to my love" beautifully inscribed, stopped him for a moment. His palms were sweaty. His heart beat a bit faster. The tears were back. He sat there as the north wind made its presence known. He'd been good all day. He made it through and carried on traditions. But deep inside, there was emptiness. Santa told him nothing but time could fill it. The scent of lilac mingling with lavender filled his soul. It was as if Abbey was sitting next to him. After a few minutes, Steve lifted the envelope out of the box and gently opened it.

With strength gathered from that little boy waiting for his daddy to come home to the husband sitting in the shadows as his wife lie dying; Steve sat back and began reading.

> *My darling Steve,*
> *As I sit in the stillness of the night looking out beyond the pasture, I see you in every star twinkling. In my twilight hour, I lean on you for strength and solace. Even though cancer has taken my hair, crippled me with pain, left me hollow in disease, and will soon extinguish my presence on this earth, it can never destroy my love for you.*

You've blessed me, my darling, with patience and understanding, laughter, and acceptance. You pushed me beyond my self-induced limits and encouraged me to face demons from my past. Because of you, I am whole.

Although I leave you, I'm going nowhere. Although I'm silent, you'll hear me whisper through the trees. Do not grieve, my darling. Laugh and love. Share and go on because I am in the wind and snow. I'll blossom in the flowers. I'll spread my wings and reach beyond the mountaintops.

I wish you a Christmas of peace and joy and for every Christmas hereafter the realization that there does exist within us as adults that magic and wonder of the season that beat within us as children. You are my believer. You are my dreamer. And now, you are the reindeer keeper's helper.

To say I love you is inadequate. Knowing you love me will stay with me throughout time.

Your Abbey

Holding the letter close, Steve walked over to the far window. Abbey's canvas stretched about the woods and pasture and beyond the timberline. Steve turned and looked at the tree. His tears were now of serenity, not sorrow. He put the letter back into the envelope and then placed it with that other letter into the wooden box with painted flowers. On top of the letters Steve placed the ribbons. He unplugged the lights and took the box with him up the back stairs to bed.

With winter's light coming through the windowpanes, Steve opened the top drawer of his nightstand. He took out Abbey's obit that had been carefully cut out of the paper. He placed it inside the wooden box holding two ribbons, a letter to Santa, and a love letter. Then he set the box down on the nightstand. Pulling the old quilt around him, Steve watched glistening snowflakes fall quietly out of sight.

From somewhere came the memory of a high school dance taking place in a gym after a football game. They'd beaten their most fervent rivals. They were going to the playoffs. The student body was wound right up with every female desperately wanting to be the one going parking with the stud of the team. But none of the miniskirted girls with heavy makeup impressed Steve. He had his eye on a girl with a ponytail standing off to the side, talking to some friends. He'd seen her in the hallways. He'd asked underclassmen her name. As the lights dimmed, it was announced this would be the last dance of the evening. That's when Steve walked past the flirting throng and past friends urging him to pick up the hot blonde with the hoop earrings. He knew where he was going. His heart had decided long before speaking to her.

"Would you like to dance, Abbey?" asked the captain of the football team.

Oblivious of anyone around them, they melted into one as Elvis told them you can't help falling in love. They couldn't. There was no explanation necessary. Later in the crisp night air, they sat on the steps of the funeral home, talking as if they'd been together forever.

Now they were. Now as the train wailed beyond the mountains and the reindeer keeper turned off the lights in the barn, that young couple's love was written through all eternity.

Seven Months Later

AT PRECISELY SIX TWENTY-NINE ON THE morning of July 3, after fourteen plus hours of labor, Greta Elizabeth Williams was born. She weighed eight pounds nine ounces and was twenty-one inches long. Steve had driven Meg to the hospital. She'd been in the garden picking green beans when her water broke. He took the back roads. He'd done the same thing when Abbey went into labor three weeks premature with Sam.

"We'll make better time," he'd told Meg.

He had no clue if this was true or not. He was trying to sound reassuring, as if he had the situation under control. One thing he was certain of was Abbey's presence. Around every curve, even as he pulled up onto the emergency room ramp, he felt her guiding him.

Eric arrived as Meg's obstetrician was examining her. He never left her side. He rubbed her back and fed her ice chips. He supported her. He knew when to say nothing. He never flinched. He never missed a contraction as one roared into the next. He wiped her forehead and reminded her to breathe. Eric was Meg's strength, just as Steve had been Abbey's. When the doctor told Meg to push, Eric knew the time was near.

"You can do this, Meg. Push, honey. Push with all your might."

And she did. Bearing down, drenching wet, and shaking in pain, Meg found strength straight from heaven. As morning awakened, she let out one final groan, leading to a beautiful baby girl crying. Eric couldn't stop the tears. He couldn't stop telling Meg how much he loved her as they held their newborn, perfect from head to toe.

Sam and Cate were home for the holiday. They'd been pacing about the waiting room with Steve, drinking cold coffee and watching the clock. Now standing with Eric in front of the nursery, not one of them noticed the man standing nearby. Even when he spoke, they didn't realize he was speaking to them.

"What a beautiful baby. She reminds me of her grandmother when she was born; lots of hair with a bit of color to her cheeks; same definition in the lips. Bet she'll have brown eyes."

Steve assumed the man making those remarks was with others standing at the window; talking about another baby. But when he heard the words "grandmother" and "brown eyes" in one sentence, he looked over at the stranger, who really wasn't a stranger at all.

"Jack! Where did you come from? How did you know we were here?" Steve grabbed hold of Abbey's brother.

Jack couldn't stop crying. It took him a moment before he could speak and when he did his voice was cracking. "She was always there for me. Abbey was my other half."

"As she was mine, Jack. Abbey would be pleased you're here to share this moment with us."

"I am so sorry I couldn't get home for her funeral Steve. I am so very sorry."

"Abbey tended to every detail."

"She took after Dad. I can't believe I've lost them both."

"Now we've been given Greta. It's the cycle of life and Abbey understood that more than most."

"Yes she did." Jack moved closer to Steve and spoke in a whisper, "I remember how Abbey never cared for the name Greta. She was thankful that was not her middle name."

"She broke down those barriers, Jack. Once she did, even that name was acceptable."

"I'm glad she found peace with Mom before she died."

"If he only knew the whole story," thought Steve, watching his grand-daughter stretch. "Greta does look like her grandmother Jack. It's the shape of her head; the way her lips part."

By now the boys knew who this man was. He'd changed since they'd last seen him; he was heavier with a little less hair. But he had a great tan.

"Congratulations, Eric. What a beautiful baby!" Jack pulled Eric in for a bear hug. "Your mother told me you and your wife had moved back. More than once, she told me how much she appreciated everything you both did for her; said she couldn't have gotten through it without you."

Jack turned to Sam and did the same. "And you, Sammy, I was watch-ing the Academy Awards. Congratulations on your nomination."

After meeting Cate, everyone followed Eric to Meg's room.

"We'll leave you two alone," said Steve after they all congratulated the new parents over and over again. "I just wanted Jack to say hello."

"How long can you stay?" asked Sam.

"I'm on my way back to the city. Have to catch a flight to Chicago."

"How did you find us? How did you know we were here?"

"You know how Abbey was, Steve. She'd given me directions in case I was ever in the area, as she put it. When I couldn't find anyone at the house, I walked around. I ended up down at your barn. Some little guy was getting out of his truck and he told me you were here. That's quite the spread. I was shocked when Abbey told me some stranger left it all to Dad. But after thinking it over, it made perfect sense."

A nurse entering the room with Greta interrupted the conversation. They were soon watching her asleep in Meg's arms.

It was Cate who first noticed another miracle. "Look! Look out the window. That can't be snow? Is that snow?"

"I've heard of Christmas in July, but I've never seen it snow in July. That is really snow! What is going on?" Jack rushed to the window.

Everyone followed. It made no sense—unless you were a believer.

Steve remembered what Abbey had written. "Do not grieve, my dar-ling. Laugh and love. Share and go on because I am in the wind and snow."

As he stood witness to the miracle with Abbey's words playing through his mind, Eric tapped him on the shoulder. "Hold your grand-daughter, Dad. Tell her about her grandmother."

And so the grandfather did. He pulled the newborn near and told her about this woman who'd love her beyond the tallest mountains, love her through every blooming flower and every whispering breeze. He told her of the snowflakes falling when they shouldn't be falling unless you understood. He told her about snow angels. He told her about those shelves of children's books waiting for her. As colored crystals mingled and fell with snowflakes in the middle of summer, Steve told his grand-daughter stories. He kept one story to himself. He knew there would be time for the reindeer keeper. He knew Greta would have her own letters to write to Santa Claus, and Abbey would be right by Santa's side, reading every word. After all, *some things are meant to be.*

Barbara Briggs Ward is the author/illustrator of *The Really, Really Hairy Flight of Snarly Sally, Snarly Sally's Garden of ABCs,* and *The Really Hairy Scary Butterfly Rescue.* Her projects include illustrating *And Then There Was Hope* and *The Brain Reigns* for the New York State Office of Mental Health. She has been a featured author/illustrator on Mountain Lake PBS in Plattsburgh, New York, and Target's Book Festival in Boston and New York City. She has been published in *Highlights for Children, McCall's,* and the *Crafts Report.* An essay led to a feature in *Ladies' Home Journal.* Her short story "In Anticipation of Doll Beds," was accepted for inclusion in Chicken Soup of the Soul's "Christmas Magic," released October 2010. She is currently a member of the Society of Children's Book Writers and Illustrators. Barbara invites you to visit www.snarlysally.com and www.thereindeerkeeper.com.

Suzanne Langelier-Lebeda is an award-winning graphic designer/illustrator. She earned national awards for art and publication design as a coordinator of publications at the State University of Potsdam. Her projects have included illustrations for the National Park Service Cumberland Island National Seashore Visitors Center, Georgia; Renee Fleming Benefit Concert Materials, New York City; Adirondack Life and Country Living Gardener Magazines; St. Lawrence University; Clarkson University; and graphic design for the permanent exhibit on History and Traditions at SUNY Potsdam. She is a member of the Adirondack Artists' Guild in Saranac Lake, New York. In her fine artwork she primarily concentrates on contemplative nature studies that explore intimations in nature by integrating watercolor, drawing, writing, and digital photography. Suzanne invites you to visit www.snowlinedesign.com.

Made in the USA
San Bernardino, CA
03 December 2013